PRAISE FOR

THE BARRY ROSS
INTERNATIONAL MYSTERIES

by ANN LIVESAY

"An environmental James Bond, impervious to danger, devastatingly attractive to females, a man of action and intelligence...Excellent format which makes the reading easy as well as great fun!"

Margaret Baker, *Baldwin Ledger* (Kansas)

What could be more romantic and exciting than a murder high up in the Himalayas?...*THE MADMAN OF MOUNT EVEREST* is a combination of mystery and fascinating journey into a culture closed to most of humanity. Livesay creates a powerful backdrop, which is an end unto itself."

Midwest Book Review

"A stalker novel, but one which includes a very different twist, beginning with a body torn apart by what the natives swear is a yeti, an abominable snowman. The peoples, sights, smells of Yogyakarta, Java, along with the cold, snow and thin atmosphere of the Nepalese mountain tops provide a travelogue backdrop to this pursuit of a mad killer."

I Love a Mystery

THE CHALA PROJECT:
MURDER IN THE GRAND CANYON

A Barry Ross International Mystery

by Ann Livesay

Silver River Books
Medford ○ Boise ○ San Francisco

This Silver River Book contains
the complete text of the original novel.

THE CHALA PROJECT:
MURDER IN THE GRAND CANYON
A Barry Ross International Mystery

First Edition August 2001
All Rights Reserved.

For information address:
Silver River, Inc., 1619 Meadowview Drive, Medford, OR 97504,
USA.   silverriv@aol.com
The Silver River web site address is http://www.silverriver.com

Library of Congress Catalog Card Number: 99-072822

ISBN 0-9662817-3-X

PRINTED IN THE UNITED STATES OF AMERICA

10 9 8 7 6 5 4 3 2 1

Also in this Series
The Isis Command
Death In the Amazon
The Madman of Mount Everest
(in preparation):
The Dinkum Deaths: Murder on the Great Barrier Reef

Foreword

In 1949, I applied to the Chief Naturalist of Glacier National Park, Montana, for a summer job, and was turned down flat. Though a Phi Beta Kappa graduate *summa cum laude* in geology from the University of Illinois, and a geologist at the Illinois State Museum (quite good credentials, I thought, for lecturing to the public) I had another problem. I was female. "We have never had a woman on the park ranger staff of Glacier National Park," wrote the Chief Park Naturalist, "and doubtless we never will."

Not giving up easily, I wrote to Louis Schellbach, Chief Park Naturalist of Grand Canyon National Park in Arizona, and was welcomed with open arms.

Thus began a long association with the Grand Canyon. In the ensuing years, I gave hundreds of rim talks, nature walks, and campfire programs, and hiked down into the canyon many times. The toughest trip was by trail from the North Rim down to the river, and up to the South Rim on the Kaibab Trail—21 miles in all—in midsummer. The most beautiful trip was down into the canyon of the Havasupai Indians in spring, when the western redbud trees and stream orchids were in full bloom.

Without question, though, the most rousing and adventurous trip was 200 miles down the Colorado River on a pontoon raft with ten other people. From Lee's Ferry, at the northern end, all the way to Lava Falls, at the western end, we were on the river for six days and nights in June. We sank into or skewed and danced across the tops of violent rapids at least twenty times every day. While the water, fresh out of the bottom of Lake Powell, was 47 degrees F. (decidedly icy to the touch), the days and nights were blistering. We crawled into tents on the beaches each evening for protection from the incessant sands hurled by canyon breezes. And then into, or onto, a sleeping bag when the temperature of 100 degrees lasted until 3 a.m. Some people preferred to dip a towel into the icy water and then crawl under that to sleep, but I never found that much of a solution because it didn't take long for the towel to reach 100 degrees.

Yet that is one of the last great adventures in North America. Since then, I have wanted to share it with readers strong enough to absorb a dose of murder and suspense at the same time.

I shall never forget the debt I owe Louis Schellbach, not only for daring to hire a female on his staff, but sharing with me the benefit of a lifelong love of the canyon country. The assistant superintendent, Lon Garrison, a writer himself, took pride in my pioneering the role of women in protecting natural resources. He wrote an article, illustrated with a picture of me in uniform on the rim, that appeared in the Phoenix, Arizona *Republic*. Indeed, I owe much to the wonderful staff at the park.

All the while thoroughly humbled by what I consider the greatest natural spectacle on earth. And pretty dangerous, too...

Ann Livesay

A NOTE TO THE READER FROM BARRY ROSS

In *The Isis Command* we followed Julie down the Nile in a felucca, lashed by terrorists to a load of high explosives. I got a lot of questions about how we came to know this very brave woman. Rejoice! The answer is at hand.

To me, it is an epic answer, for I have never known anyone so kind and gentle and brilliant, and as tough as nails, mentally and physically. She has to be understanding to be a United States park ranger. She has to like people. And in her job as inner canyon ranger at Grand Canyon National Park, as you are about to see, she sometimes has to be as tough as the quartz veins in the Vishnu Schist at the bottom. For when someone goes over a ledge and falls thousands of feet, she has to go pick up the remains. If she can find them. If she can get there. If she...

The story that follows may require at times that you fasten the seat belt in your rocking chair. Better do it. I am going to give you this story straight, and I don't want you to fall out. I have had to piece this story together from what others have related to me because it takes place at various locations within the Canyon. You'll understand.

Meanwhile, there are readers still berating me for delaying the story of the Dinkum Deaths on the Great Barrier Reef. Cheer up. That's next.

Barry

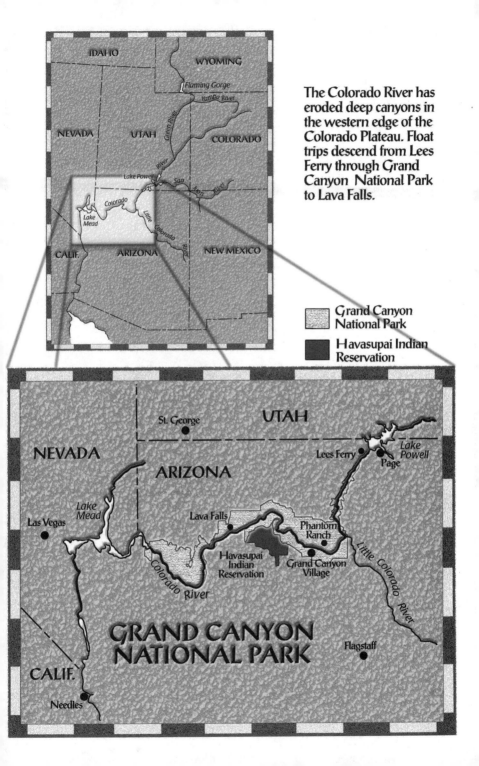

The Colorado River has eroded deep canyons in the western edge of the Colorado Plateau. Float trips descend from Lees Ferry through Grand Canyon National Park to Lava Falls.

Grand Canyon National Park

Havasupai Indian Reservation

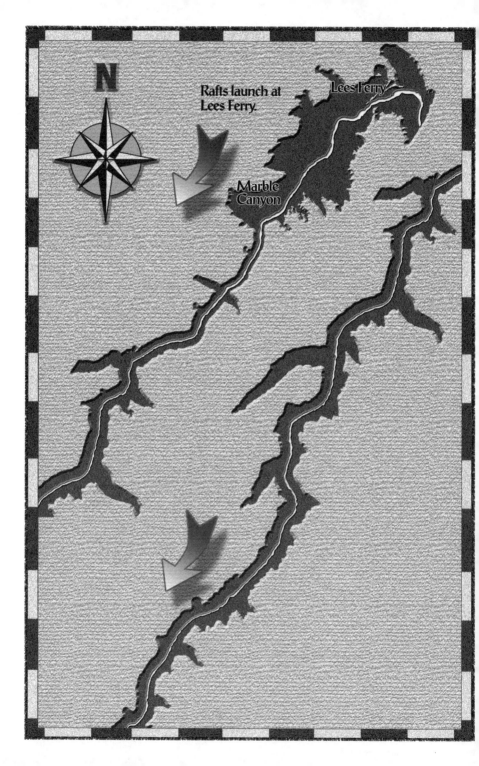

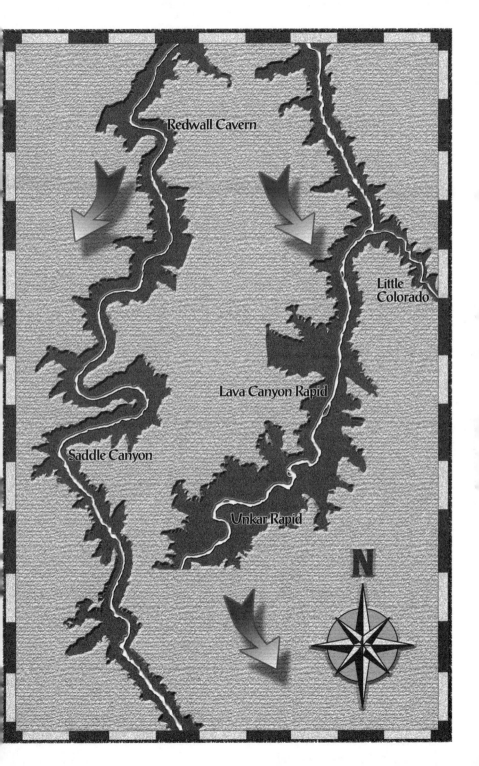

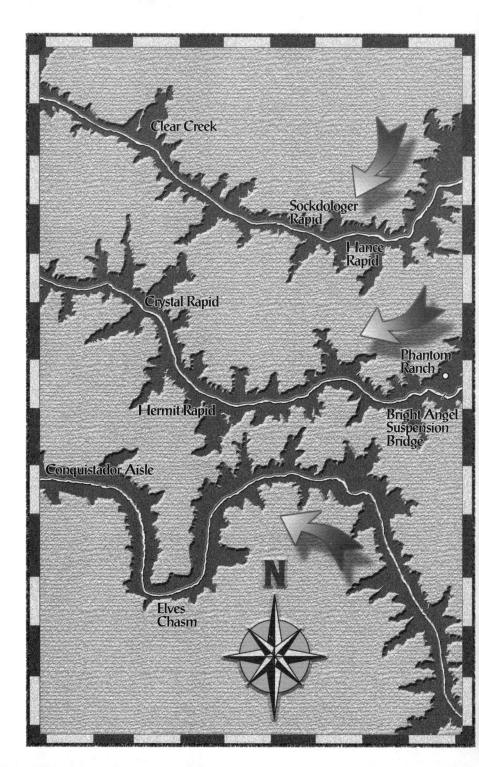

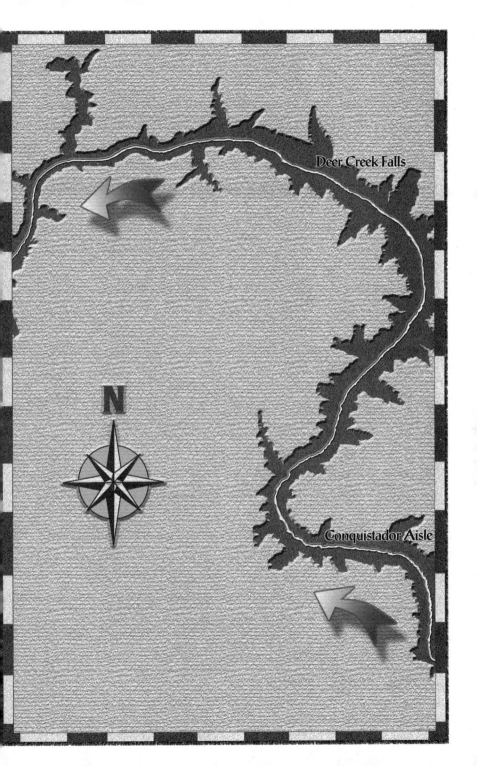

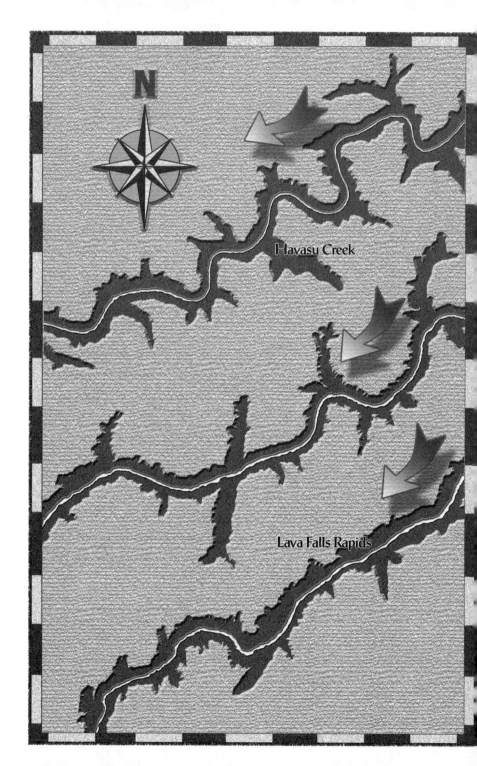

Chant with joy
At the wonders
Of this marvelous
And holy doctrine
That was made
For man and beast.

Tibetan chant c. 900 B.P.

Julie Baxter fell over the edge, slid down the slabby slope, hit a small piñon tree and grasped its trunk, her feet dangling out over five thousand feet of open space.

A slab of Coconino sandstone, dislodged as she tumbled, sailed over the edge and fell three hundred feet before it hit the slope of the Hermit shale, bounced from ledge to ledge of the Supai formation, shattered and disappeared over the edge of the five-hundred-foot cliff of the Redwall limestone.

Julie watched, fascinated. Had she fallen, she would have been knocked unconscious on hitting the Hermit shale and been battered by each successive ledge of the Supai. Little of her body would have been left to go over the Redwall.

She didn't watch long. Not with her legs dangling in space and only a straggly piñon holding her back.

To get solid footing on an undercut cliff she had to push her boot inward and heave herself outward for a better hold on the little tree trunk. She let go with one hand and grasped a bit farther up on the trunk.

Another push inward. Another bounce outward. A higher grasp on the little trunk which began to sag under her weight and bend a little farther downward.

She glanced at the roots of the tree, embedded in a crevice. Not a secure place for any tree to start. Soil, roots and tree could rip out of there without warning.

Another push. Another bounce. This time Julie managed to grasp the lip of a small rocky crevice. Not much, but it seemed a more solid hold than the tree.

Or did it? How could a slabby rock made up of tiny sand grains blown across a vast Permian desert two hundred and fifty million years ago support much weight? The soft sands had been compressed over the years by the weight of rock layers subsequently deposited on top of them and since removed by erosion. The resulting sandstone remained friable, fractured, unevenly cross-bedded. Not much to inspire confidence in mountaineers.

Granite you could trust. Usually. But clinging to a cliff of sandstone is taking a real chance.

Julie knew that. She and all the other rangers at the park had studied the geology of the Grand Canyon in their initial training. They knew every layer that made up the walls. Every kind of rock. Every outcrop along the trails.

As inner canyon patrol ranger, Julie lived with each layer, hiked the trails across their exposed faces, watched with binoculars as swifts and swallows soared above the ledges and swooped in graceful glides to their nests.

Julie therefore dared not trust all her weight on the crevice into which she had managed to get the tips of her fingers.

She pulled. Nothing happened.

She pulled a little harder. No sound of cracking rock.

She tested her weight. Still nothing. The piñon tree gripped by her other hand cracked again, giving way slightly.

All right. The handhold in the Coconino *seemed* solid. She might be able to make the transfer.

She had better do it fast. The little piñon tree weakened, loosened...

Wait no longer. She pulled with all her might, got a boot sole against the tree trunk and thrust herself upward. The tree pulled out of the crevice in which it had grown and sailed off the cliff into open space.

She came down against the loose, slipping slabs of the Coconino, fingertips in a crevice, boot braced against a slab. A loose slab that could go at any moment.

She paused to catch her breath.

Where open space, a moment before, lay directly beneath her feet, now it lay a ledge away—but with no piñon to break her fall if the slab came loose.

She had to get out of there.

She looked up. No going back the way she'd fallen. Too steep to climb. Too smooth. No hand holds. No tree trunks. Only a tiny talus slope of broken slabs, one of which she had sent over the edge in her initial fall. She hoped no one had been below...

Typical of Julie...to think of someone else at a time like this. The cardinal rule in this canyon remained: never throw anything over the edge for fear of hitting someone below. And in her fall she had done just that, dislodged rocks and gravel. She couldn't help it—but the damage had been done. Even a small rock, falling thousands of feet, could kill someone down there.

She looked around again. Nothing level surrounded her. This tiny cul-de-sac, enclosed by broken walls, had a rock-strewn pitching floor that fell away to the open space inches away. If she tried to crawl to the west, she would have to cross the broken slabs, any one of which could slide away and pitch her off.

To the east lay some possibilities. The crevice she clung to angled down in a smooth line that represented the solidified surface of an ancient sand dune. It joined a cliff not quite so vertical as the one to the west, a cliff she might be able to climb around and seek safety on the other side. Once again, though, as she could tell from here, she would have to do it hanging by her fingertips in open space.

Julie's eyes followed the crevice very carefully. She concluded that it would be solid all the way and—maybe—not break away as she crawled along it. By the time it reached the east cliff, it closed. If she got that far, she would have to find something else to grasp...

Scrutinizing the promontory, she saw a rough ridge above, but scarcely large enough to grip with anything more than her fingertips.

What about her boots? She studied the cliff again. A small ledge below might be enough to hold the toes of her boots. Nothing more.

Okay. The final question. Should she trust a toe-and-fingertips escape route?

Naval Tactics. She'd read a biography of the British Admiral Horatio Nelson. She remembered his battle against the Spanish off Cape Trafalgar. How strange that his life would flash through her mind now. Yet that famous dictum of decision-making in the height of battle had been printed on her mind *The moment of invention is the moment of execution.*

She gripped the crevice, pulled her foot from the treacherous slab, and worked her way on all fours toward the promontory. Gradually, she rose, placed the tips of her boots on the tiny ledge below and the tips of her fingers in the narrow crevice above. She leaned inward, stomach as flat against the rock as she could manage. But still a precarious angle. With little to grip, a gust of wind might upset her delicate balance.

In this position she must work her way out again over open space and around the promontory. She tried not to think of what could happen. Tried to forget the perspiration streaming down her brow. Tried to forget her clammy hands.

Out she went, toward the edge of the promontory. The cliff to which she clung fell backward about twenty degrees from vertical. She hugged it like a magnet. Gravity had a *little* inward pull on her. Not much. She placed her fingers

inch by inch along the crevice, moved her boot tips inch by inch along the ledge.

She looked down.

That brought up all the clichés. *Never look down. What do you think about when you slip, pitch over the edge, fall free? Does your life flash before you on the way down? You'd have a lot of time to think during a fall into the Grand Canyon. Going down is not the problem. It's the landing you'd have to worry about. The fall would be fun ...*

All that stuff. Oddly, she found the depths as beautiful from here, barely clinging over open air, as she had found them anywhere else. The afternoon sun gilding the cliffs, the zephyrs of air stirring ... A swift flying by on sleek black wings, swooping past at a hundred miles an hour, soaring down and down...

She thought of how some first-time visitors approached the rim of this famous gorge and turned, yes, green. Tinged with purple under the eyes. She'd seen it. The closer they'd gotten to the rim, the more their knees failed. They would find a bench, sit down, struggle to breathe at seven thousand feet, as though the heights paralyzed their lungs and torso and brain. No matter that a wall of concrete and rock and a metal railing separated them from the abyss. They became ill, unable to speak, unable to move.

Acrophobia did that. The fear of heights gripped many a visitor, sometimes unexpectedly. "When I saw all that space," one visitor told her, "I didn't fall back. I felt an urge to fall *forward!* Can you believe that?"

"Yes, I can," she'd said. "Happens all the time."

"It was the most frightening experience of my life."

Others had merely told their families: "Not on your life! *I'm not getting out of this car. I'm not going near the edge!*"

People *did* fall. Children walked the *railing* that was supposed to protect them from a thousand-foot drop. Photographers asked their relatives to "back up one more step." They did, and fell off.

Foolish tenderfeet walked alone on old historic trails that the National Park Service no longer maintained...remote trails strewn with rocks on which one misstep could send them pitching off.

Julie knew. As inner-canyon ranger she had had her chances to reach the remains of those who had gone down. Scrape them from the rock, pack them in a bag, bring them out on a mule. Not pretty. She seldom talked about it. It went with the job.

And if the unfortunate victim landed on a ledge too hazardous for Julie or her colleagues to reach ? For anyone to reach—? Would a ranger's life be imperiled just to bring back the fragments of a corpse?

Her lips stayed sealed.

So now, from her forward perch, she could look down. Thousands of feet, all the way to the Colorado River. An open space so vast, so empty, she could *feel* it. Hear the faint sounds of breezes strumming the piñon branches like violins. Hear the diving swifts zooming past, cleaving the air.

Flat against the cliff, she still thought of this canyon as the most beautiful, peaceful place on earth. Between summer seasons as a ranger, she could hardly teach geology at the University of Kentucky. Her mind wandered back to these walls. Her vision blurred. She loved the green grass and white fences and racing stallions of Kentucky not less...but this canyon more...

She had come for another summer. More breathtaking assignments. Overjoyed to be appointed at last to the inner canyon, looking forward to the Chala project. That would be something different. Utterly different.

Her fingers at last grasped the edge of the promontory and explored up over it. Perhaps by stretching a little, very slowly, very carefully, she could see beyond.

She planted her boot on the ledge, rose and looked over.

The little ledge for her feet *did* go on. The fingertip crevice continued.

Where these breaks in the sandstone reached another rock face, however, lay only a shelf of sandstone in a narrow chimney.

If she could get to the end of the current crevice—still a sizeable if—she would have to jump about four feet, out over open space...working her way up the chimney, with nothing in the bottom of it to catch her if she fell.

Should she try it? She *had* to try it. If she didn't, no one would know who had pushed her. Everyone would be led to believe that she had died in a most unfortunate accident. A freak accident. The mules. The pack train. She *must* climb back up. Lee must be informed immediately. And Buck, and Barry, and B.J... And, not the least, Joe in Supai...he the most in danger.

The moment of invention...

Hugging the promontory, which for a short distance became more vertical, she moved with excruciating slowness around it.

Her face, flushed with effort and anxiety, had turned red. A beautiful face. A ruggedly handsome face. Framed in close-cropped brown hair. Brown eyes in which one perceived the wisdom of the scholar and the determination of a fighting woman, testing every step, every finger hold...

She almost said to herself: "I'm going to get across this goddammed slope if it's the last thing I ever do," but thought better of it.

Mostly, Julie Baxter didn't think; she worked. Toe by toe. Fingertip by fingertip.

Fear gripped her, made her fingers almost numb. Good! As she'd been told during public speaking instruction in the ranger academy, "Getting up on a stage before a hundred or a thousand people, terrifies the best of speakers. It clears the mind. You *ought* to be scared!"

The echoes of those words reassured her as she slowly crossed the cliff face, heels still hovering over empty air, fingers still clutching the barest of crevices.

Finally, the last ledge. From here she must crouch like a mountain lion—which she dared not do because she hadn't enough room in which to make a maneuver like that.

She would have to let her lower legs and calf muscles provide the burst of power. But they were so tired, so numb. As much trail hiking as she'd done, she ought to have the power she needed.

She'd have only one chance to find out.

She scanned the ledge, the chimney, the overhang above, the opposite wall of this new cul-de-sac, the lone juniper on the rim over there...out of reach.

"You have to jump," she said to herself. "The moment of invention, Remember? You're not going back. *You have to jump.*"

So saying...

The Chala Project bugged me right from the start. I would have turned it down in a flash if there had been any way to get out of it. But Chala was an old friend of mine. What else could I do?

I loved the canyon and didn't mind going down the Colorado River. I had a helluva time trying to get away. The Mño crisis was brewing in Venezuela and they were screaming for help. I'd just gotten a call from San Francisco about an ominous situation in Yosemite National Park. Not to mention Tongariro, Galápagos, and the problems down on Lake Huechulaufquen in Argentina.

Ferrying someone down the river wasn't exactly my thing, but this whole business was being painted as an international crisis-in-the-making. And who else could defuse it? Me, Barry Ross, international criminal investigator, miracle maker. Phooey! I never had a bag of miracles, and I didn't now.

It was all wrong. Of all the places to try to get a VIP through safely, the Grand Canyon would be last on the list. When I arrived at the Park last March to meet with Superintendent Thomas and his staff, Julie was there. So was Buck Stevens, river ranger. Chala would take place mostly below the rim.

I opened the meeting. "Gentlemen, Hounto Chala, a West African official of the United Nations Environment Programme, has always wanted to come to Arizona to visit Grand Canyon National Park."

Thomas, white-haired, tall, fatherly, and amiable, sagged in his chair. "This is for entertainment?"

"Not quite," I replied. "His field is wildlife, and he has done a lot for world animal populations. That has led him into the field of natural reserves in which the animals live. He wants your people to tell him how it's done in America."

Thomas stroked his chin. "We can do that here on the rim."

My shoulders sagged. "I wish we could."

Buck Stevens asked sharply. "Then why not?"

I sighed. "Gentlemen, this is a very black, very important African dignitary. What he says is listened to by half the world. That is enough for both the State and Interior Departments to issue orders that we dare not corrupt."

Thomas: "Why not Everglades? That's a biological reserve. Florida is closer to Africa than the Grand Canyon."

I continued: "Well, I think you're familiar with travel statistics that show the Grand Canyon among the top ten destinations of overseas visitors to the U.S.A. He knows all about you. He probably has every travel brochure his staff can find."

"Does he know what time of year he's asking for? Does he know how busy we are in summer?"

I shook my head helplessly. "That's exactly when he wants to come. See you in full action. It all adds up. I can't help it. He's one of the best friends of conservation. The UN doesn't think we can turn him down. Neither does State."

Thomas let a helpless look cross his face. "If they were in my place, they might have second thoughts."

"Why?" I asked.

The superintendent looked out the window at the pinyon pine forest. "Our staffing is tighter than usual this summer, what with budget cuts. I realize that it is our job to take eminent visitors on tours. But six days on the river is a major undertaking. And this guy comes with security problems."

Buck added: "Bad security problems."

I couldn't argue with any of this. "That's my job."

"Easy for you to say that," Buck replied with a sigh. "But there are thousands of canyons within this canyon. Thousands of hiding places. A rifle behind one of them. And you don't know which. You will need a lot of ranger help, and summer is our busiest time. The rangers are needed elsewhere. Mind you, Barry, I'm not bitching. We just want to do the best job we can, and it's going to be tough as hell. The CIA has informed us that international assassins have marked Chala for elimination. Is that true?"

I nodded.

"What for?"

I waited a moment, then decided to let them have it point blank.

"Because he has a proposal that half the world will rejoice about and the other half will want to kill him for."

Buck responded grimly. "And anyone else standing next to him."

Julie spoke: "What could be so earth-shaking about this guy? What is he trying to do?"

I answered forthrightly. "We are losing animal life on this planet at such a rate that we are going to have silent forests before a few more generations pass. Generations in Africa, Asia, everywhere. He has a proposal that will cut all that and save the world's wildlife."

Buck reared back in his seat. "Pardon my being skeptical, Barry. One man is going to do all that?"

I then spent five minutes describing the Chala project. They listened in silence, their faces awestruck. When I finished, they were nearly unable to speak.

Julie shook her head and said softly: "This is coming from some other part of the universe. I can't believe it."

I responded promptly. "I can. Most other people of the world can. Do you know that?"

She answered. "I'm not Hindu."

Thomas: "Well, Barry, I can tell you that it's a very chilling piece of information for the superintendent of a park with millions of visitors every year. A park with river traffic especially heavy in summer. Gunfire in the midst of all this? Assassins circulating among thousands of tourists at dozens of locations? Such a nightmare no park official could ignore."

I acknowledged the delicacy of this matter.

Thomas continued: "I protested to my superiors in the regional office. Can't the guy come in September or April, or some less busy time of year? Weather's nicer, too."

Answer: No, doesn't fit into his schedule. He won't be in the US very long this time. He has to go back to Nairobi.

Thomas: "Well, then, how about down the San Juan, the Green, the Dolores? Places more wild? Other rivers just as—."

*He doesn't **want** to go down the San Juan, the Green, or the Dolores. He wants to go down the Colorado. Through the Grand Canyon. He's never even **heard** of the San Juan, the Green, and the Dolores.*

"I can't help that," Thomas pleaded. "I have a park to run. We'll be starting the summer travel season. I'm responsible for the safety of visitors every day. I don't want a field of battle popping up in the midst of all this."

*Okay, he's a visitor. Take good care of him. **Very** good care. Is that clear?*

"I don't want killers running around among those visitors. Someone could get hurt."

*If we have to **order** you to do it...*

"No, that won't be necessary. I know when I'm licked."

All I could say was that I sympathized and that in his position I would have done the same thing. The assistant superintendent, Woody Watkins, bespectacled, in his late thirties, piercing black eyes, asked: "Who *is* this guy?"

I answered in an even tone. "About all I can say at this point is that he's a Very Important Person. Very Important African. Very Important Black. That's all we need to know for the present."

Art Thomas swiveled in his chair and looked outside again. "Does he know the risk he's taking. Lifelong dream, they tell me."

Watkins snorted. "He wants to *die* here."

I shrugged. "He doesn't want to die anywhere. It's our job to see that he especially doesn't die here. The international perception is that the U.S., with all its powers, should be able to take perfect care of *anyone*."

Big Lee Federico pounded a heavy fist on the table, his brown eyes flaring. "Oh, shit! We're humans like anyone else. We're not magicians."

Art Thomas smiled and lifted his white eyebrows in a gesture of despair. "I told them that, Lee. God knows I tried. But I was run over by a freight train called the Department of State, and a landslide called the Department of the Interior."

"All right. But this is going to cost money. We'll need lots of help. Experienced help. We'll have to pull some of our own rangers off their regular duties, let the seasonals take over. We'll have to import rangers from nearby parks and monuments. That's expensive. It can't come from my budget. What if something else happens in the park while all this is going on? Anyway, who's paying for this?"

"He is."

"Chala?"

"He's rich. Oil revenues. Just get the help you need and we'll forward the bill."

Art Thomas turned and looked around the table. "I received a call direct from the Secretary of the Interior. The conversation lasted less than a minute. Art, he said, I've heard from State and the CIA. If you let any harm come to a West African prince while he is in the Grand Canyon, the U.S. will be in deep trouble. And so will you."

That had been six weeks ago. Now, on the first of June, at Lee's Ferry, in the eastern extremity of the park, Joe Muck, my assistant, an amiable young cowboy in a big straw hat, and I waited with canyon staff and borrowed rangers. For weeks, we and they had thought of little else than Hounto Chala.

We had gone to Nairobi to help plan the trip, and maybe talk him out of it? No way. The racial thing was never very far away and I understood and respected that. I wanted to do this for him in tribute to all he was doing for wildlife. It was just the timing.

With the Canyon flooded with people, whoever wanted to shoot him would be able to hide so that we'd never see him.

That didn't worry Chala. "Pas un autre mot," he said, wagging his finger elegantly. Not another word about it.

Now, in a few moments, he and his entourage would arrive under tight security, of course—and the river trip would begin.

Considering what he proposed, I could imagine a thousand determined assassins out there trying for just one potshot at him. He was big and heavy, but a bullet could go through him just as effectively as through anyone else.

This was almost approaching a nightmare.

And a nightmare for all the rangers, too. They would age prematurely before this was over.

And yet, I have to say in all modesty that had it not been for us, the task of park officials would have been much tougher. Joe and I had overseen all the arrangements, paid the costs, helped set up the personnel. Once the UN and CIA got Chala here to Lee's Ferry, starting point for nearly all Grand Canyon river trips, I would take over. I had been charged by the UN to get Chala through this canyon and out again without harm. Another layer of bureaucracy, perhaps, but the buck stopped with me.

"You'll never make it!" said Chief Ranger Lee Federico, bluntly, as we stood beside the placid Colorado River on an overcast morning. A bulky man, scarred, wrinkled, sunburnt, dark glasses hiding his eyes, Federico wasted no words. "Don't get your hopes up, Barry. Everybody in all three rafts will be a sitting duck."

I nodded, with a frown of resignation. "I know that, Lee."

"The canyon," he went on, "has a million hiding places. Anyone could take aim at this guy—from a hidden ledge or behind a tree—high up, and disappear from sight. There isn't a goddammed chance that you could catch the bastard."

He was an overpowering guy, and I felt humble in his presence and with knowledge of what he was responsible for. I was also muscular but shorter and leaner, clad as usual in Levis, sage shirt, and baseball cap. I didn't care. I wasn't trying to outshine anyone. I smiled. "Maybe so, Lee, but I

have one helluva lot of tricks up my sleeve. We're going to have to try like hell!"

Lee went on. "I know, Barry. You've been all over the goddammed globe and fought tougher situations than this. And you've been down this canyon a couple of times. So you ought to know what the hell you're doing. But how can you fight this?"

"Fight what? The hiding places?"

"Yes. This whole thing is impossible."

"I'm not going to fight them, Lee."

"Anyone could hide in them. You know that. We can't control every human being who comes into this canyon. Nobody could. Nobody. You know that, too."

"Yes I do."

The chief ranger spat on the sand beside the Colorado River. "I warn you again. This is a busy time of year for us. I could hardly find a handful of rangers from other parks to help. Zion, Bryce, Canyonlands, Arches... Those places have already got all the summer visitors they can handle. They screamed to high heaven."

I shrugged. "All right. So we go down the river under-protected. We just have to be more careful."

Lee shook his head. "Barry, I'll give you one last piece of advice. The Colorado River's crawling with people. There was no way we could close down the whole goddammed canyon just so this guy could go through safely."

I spread my hands. "I know. That request came from stupid staff work. I told them not to try that."

"You'll be surrounded by people. Floaters, rafters, the whole lot. You'll have every type of vessel comin' at you. Rafts, rowboats, canoes, kayaks. Christ, we've got people goin' down this dangerous river in anything that floats ... even *swimming* down it. Some of them are pretty weird honchos. They let themselves go. Look like hell. But this is one place where it's perfectly all right to do that. All we can do is limit the numbers. They got to have a permit. We can't screen 'em for hit squads or assassins. You're raw, Barry. Vulnerable. Open to anything."

I put my hand on Federico's arm. "We'll keep our eyes on everything, Lee. Day and night. You've done your best. I know you have. We all appreciate that very much. It would have been impossible without you and Art and Woody, all of you. Can't thank you enough. From here on it's my game. My total responsibility. I don't want any of your rangers hurt any more than Chala or the UN staff."

Lee asked: "Everybody briefed?"

"You heard it all. Anything I missed?"

"Just keep stressing these guys to look behind every rock, every tree trunk, and every cliff all the way up to the nearest rim. And watch every boat. Don't let any of 'em get near you."

I nodded in agreement. "Good advice, Lee."

We shook hands. "Barry, good luck. I'll be at headquarters. B. J. Pritchett, my assistant chief, will be with you. He and Julie Baxter and Buck Stevens can handle this river. They know their stuff. They got radios. They're the best of the lot. Let me know if you need anything, huh?"

He turned his head to look up the approach road.

"Oh, oh. Here they come."

The two vans came down the road, sending up a diaphanous mist of dust, and stopped in the loading area. Down river, a gaggle of tourists in a cordoned-off area clustered to watch the activities.

As soon as the vehicles stopped, two bodyguards emerged from the rear van and took up positions outside the door of the first van.

Tip Phrakonekham, a wiry, black-haired Thai in bright yellow vest, came forward to stand beside the door of the front van. Dietrich Deitemeyer, a worried German, jumped out and jogged over to shake hands with Woody Watkins, assistant superintendent and ranking park officer present, and with me. Deitemeyer spoke in a stern, businesslike manner. "Barry. Good to see you again. Everything's ready, I trust?"

"You can board any time."

Deitemeyer seemed relieved just to see me there. My reputation had spread so far around the world that my name became almost a guarantee that any situation under my direction remained under control. It didn't always, but that was the perception. I'm not modest about this. Just realistic. I had to live with it. And I usually needed this kind of reputation.

I worked alongside the UN as a private investigative officer. As such I had saved countless human beings, wild animals, historic sites, and world heritage reserves from attack and destruction. That made me so much in demand that I could only take cases of international significance. Hounto Chala fell in that category.

I asked: "Is His Excellency ready?"

"Yes." Deitemeyer turned to Watkins. "Your security arrangements are complete?"

Watkins, his ranger cap sporting the arrowhead symbol of the National Park Service, answered gently: "We'll be in three rafts. The first one will have three rangers and myself. The second raft, in which you, Phrakonekham and Chala ride, will have three park staff to supply him with information—the naturalist, historian, and assistant chief ranger. And the third raft will have three rangers plus Dr. Ross. Is that satisfactory to His Excellency?"

Deitemeyer: "I'm sure it will be quite satisfactory. Barry, are you satisfied?"

I shook my head. "Not in the slightest"

Deitemeyer tensed. "What? What?"

"An army wouldn't help in this canyon."

Deitemeyer frowned. "But Barry, I thought—."

"Dietrich, you and I went over this in detail in Nairobi. We simply cannot guarantee *anything*. The park service can't. The U.S. government can't. I can't."

"Quite so. I remember. I understand."

"That's fine, but does Chala understand? He did in Nairobi."

"Yes, I think he does. He's not afraid of the risk. He lives with it. This is something he's always wanted to do. But he wants maximum precautions."

I gave what assurance I could: "He has them. We have enough people to check every cliff, every tributary coming into the river. But you must understand...all the hiding places along this river... Well, there are millions of them. It will be very, very iffy..."

"Yes."

I asked: "Do you have word from INTERPOL?"

Deitemeyer frowned again. "Only that the hit squads are not yet aware of this trip. We got out of New York at night and I think we—how do you say it?—gave them the sleep."

"Slip. All right. But we could have local problems. The western U.S. is hunter country. A lot of people look on Chala's proposal with panic. They're sharpshooters. Whatever happens will happen fast."

Deitemeyer changed the subject. "What about the Press?"

Watkins answered: "We tried to keep this subdued, but word got out. They kept calling Art and me at park headquarters. A few small articles appeared."

"Anyone from the Press along?"

"Kathi LeClair. *Arizona Daily Sun.* Speaks French. I couldn't help it."

Deitemeyer turned angrily to me. "I thought I made it clear—."

I held up my hands. "Dietrich, no government agency can resist the Press in this country. The publishers went to Cabinet Members, Congressmen...they overrode all our protests."

"Even the Secretary of State?"

"It went that high."

"This could endanger a man's life, our whole project—."

I spread my hands in helplessness. "We told them that. But he's also a big story. I would have done that same thing they did. Anyway, the reporter will be on the third raft, not with Chala."

Deitemeyer let his shoulders slump. "That is all right. His Excellency likes to make decisions about reporters. He *does* have an ego. In his kingdom back home he's surrounded by the Press. Always promoting his ideas."

"He likes that?"

"Of course."

I shook my head. "Well, that's the problem. He wants the Press on his side. But he's naïve. He wants everybody to hear his proposal and join his crusade. A lot of people with rifles have heard about his proposal. They're up in arms, to put it mildly."

"Why? Why? Why? I'll never understand Americans! Never!"

I smiled. "Nor will I. So don't sweat it."

"Oh, well, Barry," he said, in a resigned tone. "It doesn't matter."

I snapped. "It does to us. We'll take good care of him."

Deitemeyer turned toward the river. "Shall we board?"

Watkins: "Any time."

Dietrich called over the Thai assistant to Chala. "Barry, I think you know Phrakonekham?"

We shook hands. "I do indeed. Tip, how are you?"

"Very well, Barry. I glad you are here. It makes Chala feel more secure."

"How is His Excellency?"

"Oh! He very good spirits, as always. He wishes he could speak English. He wants me to thank you very much for all you do..."

I responded: "Tell him to hold that until *after* the trip."

Phrakonekham laughed. "Jolly good. I tell him that."

Dietrich: "We're ready, Tip."

The Thai assistant stepped to the van and opened the door.

Out stepped the most imposing luminary, I'd guess, ever to grace the precincts of Lees Ferry.

Chala towered more than six feet tall, clad in sky-blue silk robes, his head covered with a cap adorned with leopard claws. His hand carried a lion's mane fly swatter, held imperiously at shoulder level. The prince's ebony black skin glowed under the bright white morning haze.

He immediately stepped over to me, saying: "Barry! Barry! Comment ça va? How do you do? English superb, ah?"

Everyone followed the African's uproarious laughter. Chala nearly crushed me in the ensuing embrace, after which I said, tugging at the brilliant silk robe: "Mon eminence, nous avons une petite problème avec ses riches, inoubliables vêtements. Est-ce qu'il y a un jump suit pour ce gran maître de la rivière?"

Chala roared with laughter at being called master of the river. Still, he knew I spoke the truth. These magnificent garments, these ceremonial robes, would not do on the river and he had better have a jump suit.

"Mais oui," answered Chala, "ces robes sont simplement pour faire un entrée royale."

I translated for the rest, grinning: "He says yes, he has a jump suit. These robes are merely to make a royal entrance."

Chala embraced me again and strode off to be fitted into his jump suit. The Entrée Royale had ended.

The three pontoon rafts outfitted for the Chala expedition nudged the rocky shore. Each had been anchored by ropes to angular boulders of red sandstone. Each raft resembled nothing more than two outsized, blunt-nosed silver canoes held together by a platform mounted between the oversized pontoons. Each raft floated catamaran-like, with baggage loaded on the central platform and covered by a silvery gray waterproof canvas lashed with sturdy ropes. These large rafts had a capacity of twenty people each, though on this trip they would hold fewer because of the weight of guns and ammunition.

Passengers would ordinarily sit on the deck in a circle, backs to baggage, facing outward. Except that many straddled the big pontoons as though to ride an imaginary silver horse down the river.

On a slightly elevated plank in the rear, beside the 200 horsepower motor, the boatman could sit, see ahead over the cargo, and handle the motor and rudder. The bulk of

equipment blocked some of his view, which merely meant that he would have to stand when the raft approached the most violent rapids, and would try to guide it like a charioteer when it plunged into a seething maelstrom.

Ted Quail, the lead boatman, blew a whistle, and the passengers moved toward the rafts. I led Chala, now encased in a jump suit, and helped him aboard.

Quail called out names. The passengers went on board and seated themselves, according to the list received by each.

Red Rock Expeditions
CHALA PROJECT:
UNITED NATIONS ENVIRONMENT PROGRAMME

Raft One, Advance Guard

Joe Muck, Assistant to Barry Ross
Woody Watkins, Assistant Superintendent, Grand Canyon National Park
Cynthia Kasbolt, Ranger, Bryce Canyon National Park, Utah
Eddie Roff, Ranger, Saguaro National Park, Arizona
Dalton Stubbs, Ranger, Organ Pipe Cactus National Park, Arizona
Kent Thomas, Regional Director, UNEP, New York
Ted Quail, Boatman in Charge, Red Rock Expeditions
Marjorie Cox, Cook, Red Rock Expeditions

Raft Two, Chala Party

Hounto Chala, Sub-Director, Special Projects, UNEP, Nairobi
Dietrich Deitemeyer, United Nations Liaison Officer, New York
Tip Phrakonekham, Assistant to the Sub-Director, UNEP
Neff Neilson, Park Interpreter/Naturalist, Grand Canyon Nat'l Park
Angel Ingebretson, Historian, Grand Canyon National Park
B. J. Pritchett, Assistant Chief Ranger, Grand Canyon Nat'l Park
Nabih Hussein, First Bodyguard, UNEP

Dominick Debenedictis, Second Bodyguard, UNEP
Jerry Elliott, Boatman, Red Rock Expeditions
Evie Lund, Nurse/Cook, Red Rock Expeditions

Raft Three, Rear Guard

Barry Ross, Special Investigator in Charge
Sam Petrie, Liaison Officer, United Nations, New York
Buck Stevens, River Ranger, Grand Canyon National Park
Julie Baxter, Inner Canyon Ranger, Grand Canyon National Park
Mozo Fernandez, Ranger, Coronado National Memorial
Dee Dunn, UN Special Projects Officer, New York
Kathi LeClair, Features Editor, *Arizona Daily Sun*, Flagstaff
Rudy Vogel, Boatman, Red Rock Expeditions
Pete Slattery, Equipment, Red Rock Expeditions

The boatman in each raft issued oversized luminescent orange life-jackets to every passenger. Next came minutes of confusion as each person tried to put one on and tighten it to size.

Joe Muck, my effervescent, irreverent assistant, stood in front of Raft One, his broad straw cowboy hat stamping him as a genuine American cowboy. His blue eyes, hiding behind sunglasses, scanned the dock. When he took off his hat to wave to Chala, his golden hair swirled in the river breeze.

Chala saw him, stood, and called in a powerful voice: "Joseph! Joseph! Cher ami! Comment ça va?"

Joe waved the hat like a lariat in greeting. "Bien! Bien, Mon Eminence. Et vous?"

Joe and I had not seen Chala since our trip to Nairobi the previous month to prepare for this trip. Joe had just come a few months before from training in Paris. His ability to speak French made him a favorite with Chala. The African prince had embraced the Wyoming cowboy as though to adopt him.

Joe, seeing the tiny hat Chala wore, called: "Vous n'avez pas un chapeau, mon ami." He pointed up. "Le soleil, c'est très, très chaud."

Joe suddenly felt surprised that no one had thought of providing a broad sun hat for Chala. The sun could be brutal, the canyon like a furnace. He said so: "Ce canyon, c'est vraiment comme une chaudière, Mon Eminence."

"Il n'y a pas un problème, Joseph," Chala called.

Not now, Joe replied, but there *will* be a problem later if their guest of honor got sunstroke.

Wasting no time, he leaped up on the pontoon and danced with delicate jumps among the passengers across to the pontoon of the second raft. As he came up to Chala, they embraced like long lost brothers. Joe gently lifted the prince's hat, gave it to Phrakonekham, took off his cowboy hat and placed it on the wide, round black head. What luck! Joe thought. It fit! He pulled the chin strap snugly so that the hat would not fly away during the wild rides ahead. Then he turned and danced back to Raft One amid shouts of "Merci! Merci!" from Chala.

As Joe sat down to the applause of the passengers, Woody Watkins reached into a pack and gave Joe a National Park Service cap with the arrowhead symbol on front. Joe fitted it in place, jumped up and called to Chala, pointing vigorously to the cap, "Je suis un ranger!" I am a ranger (pronouncing it *rawn-zhair*, through the nose).

Chala roared, then pointed to his own new hat. "Je suis un cowboy! Bon voyage, Ranger!"

Joe called back: "Bon voyage, Cowboy!"

With that, Ted Quail blew the whistle to signal departure.

The crew disengaged ropes from rocks and gave each raft a heave, then splashed in the water and leaped up on the pontoons.

As the rafts moved out into the current, I focused on the tangle of tourists watching us depart. The kinds of people we would be meeting and mingling with the whole trip.

They all wore clothing suitable for getting wet in: swim suits, old cut-offs, torn shirts, bandana scarfs to protect the neck from the sun, floppy hats. Some wore hats that could be wrung out after every wetting.

They looked like a scurvy lot, but they were not. Some of them appeared to be in their eighties, grizzled, white-haired, and just as excited as all the rest. Others seemed robust and powerful, unshaven, unkempt, ready to assassinate anyone who came within range.

Now you are obsessed, said my inner voice. *If you don't watch out, you'll have him wiped out before we leave. You can't keep this up for six days. You're going to have to let go. You have to sleep. Those people are not all killers...*

I had to agree. But then I saw someone with a pistol sneaking along behind all the rest, taking up a good position with a clear view at the black man in the cowboy hat...

Stop it! Stop it! You're having hallucinations.

There was someone creeping along behind the crowd all right, but only with a pair of binoculars in hand.

You see? Now stop it!

Julie Baxter, sitting beside me in the third raft, smiled and said: "You're looking at a killer?"

I smiled. "Of course. They're all killers."

She howled: "They are *not!*"

"All right. What do you see there?"

"They're good people. Families. Couples. Kids. Old folks. Having the times of their lives. They are not assassins."

"One of them is a killer."

She plowed a fist into my shoulder. "Will you get off that?"

"I can't."

She reproved me. "You have to. You have to take it easy in this hot environment. There's stress enough already. Besides, you have an assistant. Let him take over."

I smiled. "He takes over all the time anyway. He's the boss wherever he goes. And he's got the backbone to back it up."

She looked across at the other raft where Joe talked spiritedly across the water to Chala. "Joe Muck's quite a guy. Flamboyant, to say the least."

"Yes," I answered. "He *is* quite a guy."

"Where's he from?"

"Wyoming. Graduate of the university at Laramie. Wildlife biology."

"Not really?"

"Sharpshooter. Rodeo star."

Julie became more incredulous with each statement. "And he speaks French?"

"He has a lot of talents, Julie."

"Where did you find him?"

"First met him on a dugout canoe trip into the Amazon basin in Colombia."

"Wow!"

"Then he helped me capture a killer at the base of Mount Everest in Nepal..."

"He *must* be good," Julie observed.

"We sent him to Paris for ten months of intensive training in language, law enforcement, and international environmental law. He sometimes has uncanny instincts with regard to people. Very promising."

"Who's we?"

"My Aunt Kelly. She wants the world cleaned up by tomorrow and she has the funds to do it. So she tags the United Nations, and they tag me, and we're off again."

She shook her head in disbelief. "Sounds exciting!"

"Yeah," I sighed. "But how much excitement can a person take?"

She laughed. "I'll tell you about it some time..."

We moved out into the wide river, motors off, the rafts revolving slowly in obedience to the current. One minute we floated backward, the next, sideways. Green water swirled beneath the rafts, rippled along the pontoons and roiled in the wake.

The crowd of assassins we left behind now dispersed, getting ready to board their own rafts, or canoes, or rowboats.

For a while the valley remained wide, the river broad and shallow, the purple rims hundreds of yards away. All the better, I thought, to keep these dangerously vulnerable rafts safe from ambush.

However... Those long rows of Tamarix, or salt-cedar, along the river banks, their slender green fronds waving slowly in the soft morning breeze... They could harbor hidden

assassins... Those copses of mesquite, climbing up the troughs of dunes... In their dark shade lay many a hiding place...

As the vessels floated apart, no more than a hundred yards from one another, the boatmen in each raft seized the opportunity to lay down rules.

Rudy Vogel, hardened veteran of river trips, browned by the sun, skin furrowed and cracked by years of wind, sand, and water, left the rudder and stepped up on the cargo canvas. Adjusting his weatherbeaten, well-oiled, well-soiled hat, he squinted at the sky, the river, the passengers.

"A few rules," he drawled, "just to keep us all on the same track."

He looked down at his feet, adjusted the tobacco in his cheek, and went on. "This here's the most beautiful river on earth. But it's a mighty tricky river. Ain't no other'n like it. I don't need to tell you nothin' about them there currents. You can see fer y'se'ves. Right there. And there. Comin' up and goin' down. Jes you get a good look at 'em. That's power! They can pull you straight down and keep you there. And they has sure done that to a lot of people along this river. So we say, no swimmin' allowed till we git to camp and tell you when and where.

"The water's green here. Used to be brown. Sometimes gits brown after a cloudburst, or maybe from floods pourin' in from side creeks. You can see the high-water marks on the walls as we go down. When them boulders roll on the river bottom you can hear the loud roar. Nowadays, all them sediments this river used to carry through the canyon, and a whole lot of the boulders it used as tools to carve these here walls, ain't no longer here. They git dumped now in the upper end of Lake Powell."

The passengers watched and listened, their eyes roving from Rudy's face to the swirling waters to the Vermilion Cliffs in the distance, tinted purple in the morning haze.

"This water here came from the bottom of Glen Canyon Dam, not fur up the river. I measured the temperature this mornin'. Forty-seven degrees. On the rest of our trip, the water temperature will git up to fifty-two degrees..."

Dee Dunn, fortyish, brown hair, with a large build, interrupted. As a special projects officer with the United Nations, she had done a great deal of travel, but not on *this* river. She turned up her wide brown eyes and asked: "How are we going to *swim* in water that cold?"

"Vigorously, ma'am," Rudy replied. "Vigorously."

She turned her head away. "I dare say!"

"At first, you're only gonna git sprayed with that cold water in some of the rapids we go through," Rudy went on. "Then you're gonna git plunged in clear over your head, and get *real* soused in it. Ain't no way I can help it. You're gonna git wet. And in some of the big falls—."

"*Falls?*" asked Kathi LeClair, the news reporter. "*Water falls?*"

Rudy looked at her with a blank face. "What other kind of falls is they?"

Her blue eyes had opened wide. She wore a broad blue hat, but he could see underneath that she had suddenly become worried. "Well, rock falls," she answered. "But I didn't know there were any waterfalls on this river. I thought—."

"Well, ma'am, you can call 'em ripples if'n you want. You can call 'em rapids. I call 'em waterfalls cause that's what the water does. It falls. Of course, these waterfalls is stretched out a little, and maybe some of 'em's a little more horizontal than vertical, but I call 'em waterfalls lyin' down."

Kathi sat back and lowered her head, not quite sure she wanted to hear any more. She took out a notebook and pencil. "Rudy, you're a poet. Waterfalls lying down. I like that. Good title."

"And if you think we always go *over* the falls," Rudy added, "t'ain't always so. Sometimes we goes over 'em. Sometimes we goes *through* 'em. And sometimes we goes *under* 'em."

Kathi lowered her head even further, then looked up at Rudy and grinned. "Can I get off at the next stop?"

Dee Dunn observed: "Shivering one minute, burning the next. Is that it?"

Rudy nodded. "Most of the way we'll have a purty cool trip. That cold water cools the air just above the surface of the river. But the sun is still hot. It'll still burn."

Mozo Fernandez, the ranger of Mexican descent from Coronado National Memorial on the border between Arizona and Mexico, asked: "How many rapids are there?"

"Two hundred, more or less," Vogel replied.

Kathi LeClair's pencil stopped. She looked up. "How many?"

"If you go all the way to Lake Mead. Two hundred. Kinda depends on flood stage."

Kathi asked, with a worried frown: "Are we in flood stage?"

"No."

"Will we be?"

"Not unless we gits a cloudburst. Then look out!"

Kathi said, jokingly. "I wanna go home."

Rudy went on. "We won't see all the rapids—we leave the river before then. And sometimes the river's height depends on how much water they release from Glen Canyon dam."

Rudy stepped back to adjust the rudder, then retook his position on the baggage pile.

"We go ashore now and then for a pit stop. Only, we do things kind of different from what you're used to. To us, this place is a wilderness. We got thousands of people going through this canyon ever year. If everbody left everthing behind, it could ruin the trip for everbody else." Kathi's pencil whirred across the page. "So... Rule Number One is to take out what we bring in. All of us. That applies to body wastes, too. You can urinate in the river, but as for Number Two, we carry a potty chair. Wastes are collected in plastic bags and taken out of the canyon at the end of the trip."

"Quite right!" said Dee Dunn, clapping her hands. "A cheer for you, Rudy."

"Tain't my idea. It's regulations. Everbody has to do it. Any questions?"

Kathi spoke up. "Back to these rapids. How do we keep from being dumped in the river?"

Rudy pointed to the ropes holding down the cargo. "See them ropes? When we approach a rapid—I'll give you a warning so you can sit down and grab one of 'em."

"Then what?"

"Hang on like hell!"

The canyon walls closed in. Layer on layer of brown sandstone rose above the river. Great slabs and piles of rocky debris had fallen from the rims and walls to repose precariously on slopes below. In this talus jumble mesquite tried to grow.

The rafts came close together now. Through the thin overcast, heat from the mid-morning sun poured into the gorge. With that came our first hint of the *chaudière,* the furnace Joe Muck had warned Chala about.

In Raft One, Cynthia Kasbolt, the ranger from Bryce Canyon National Park in Utah, brushed the straight strands of her golden hair, and looked up. "This is a really dangerous part of the trip."

"How do you figure?" asked Eddie Roff, the gentle, soft-spoken ranger from Saguaro National Park.

"Anyone could hide on top there and have a clean shot at us," Cynthia replied. "Canyon's not very deep in this part of Marble Gorge. City of Page not far away. Roads to the rim. All that."

Dalton Stubbs, the pensive ranger from Organ Pipe Cactus National Park, observed: "If they know what they're doing, they'll knock off Chala here, then get away by car."

"Not so good," Cynthia responded.

"Why not?"

"We'd radio the Arizona Highway Patrol—they're standing by at the old bridge just ahead to make sure no one looks down on us—and they'd nab the guys in minutes."

"You think it's better farther on?"

Cynthia said: "Sure. They go down some remote trail. Hide in a cave. Shoot him from a cliff. Preferably while we were going through rapids so that the roar of the water would muffle the gunshot. We wouldn't have the foggiest where it came from. Then they go out by trail—a real head start. See?"

"Not if we put helicopters on 'em."

"At night? No way. By day? They just hide under a ledge. They hold the winning cards, Dalton."

Suddenly Eddie Roff, assigned to scan the right bank, signaled them to cut the conversation.

"Someone on the rim ahead," he said, "upper right."

I sat upright on full alert.

All binoculars focused on three figures atop a sandstone cliff.

Woody Watkins, Grand Canyon assistant superintendent, took up his microphone.

"B. J.?" he said, in a low voice, calling to B. J. Pritchett, the park's assistant chief ranger, in the second raft with the Chala party.

"Yes, sir?"

"Three people, top of the rim, on the right."

Pause.

Pritchett responded. "We see 'em."

Woody: "From here they look like teenagers. I don't think it's a problem. But you better get Chala down till we pass."

"Roger."

As we floated beneath the cliff on which the figures stood, we kept close watch. Suddenly, a rock sailed out into space and splashed into the river a hundred yards downstream from the first raft.

Joe Muck reached down and retrieved his H and H Magnum rifle from its rubberized case, lifted the muzzle, aimed for a cliff face a hundred yards to the left and below the teenagers. Without a moment's hesitation, he squeezed the trigger.

The sound of the shot echoed between the canyon walls, as though a platoon had commenced firing. The bullet smacked into the cliff and ricocheted with a loud ping-n-nnng!

The teenagers whirled, lunged, tripped, scrambled up a ledge and vanished.

Watkins to Pritchett: "It's okay, B. J. Playful teens getting too close. But keep an eye up there for a few minutes."

"Roger, Woody."

Watkins turned to Joe. "That was okay. But if anyone on the rim has a gun, Joe, you'll have to be a better shot."

Joe answered, putting away his rifle: "If they'd had guns I would have dropped them into the river in six seconds."

We settled back down again—but more alert than ever.

Dalton Stubbs had a puzzled look on his face. "I just don't get it. I still can't figure out why this guy is in such danger. Who's got him targeted? Why?"

Kent Thomas, a studious Canadian from Ottawa and a regional director of the United Nations Environment Programme, pulled his pipe from his mouth and responded, keeping his eyes on the cliffs.

"Chala is one of the most influential Africans alive."

"So? He's in the U.S. now."

"That makes him more influential. He's here on a special project."

"I haven't heard of him."

Kent puffed on his pipe for a moment and scanned a cliff overhead. "You will."

Stubbs adjusted his life preserver and sat back to get better views of the rims on the left, which he had been

assigned to scan. "How can a man accomplish anything if he's a constant target?"

"That's the obvious part of it."

Stubbs smiled. "Kent, you're being confoundedly enigmatic."

Kent Thomas's eyes followed the river bank, the fallen boulders, a huge sandstone chunk parting the green waters of the Colorado. "You see that rock over there? The one half submerged?"

"Yes."

"That's Chala. The world is a river that flows all around him."

"Yes?"

"But he stands in place. He doesn't flow with the rest."

Dalton Stubbs didn't think he quite caught the drift of that. "I take it you mean he's standing up against some kind of tide."

Kent mused. "Like that rock."

The sandstone boulder receded as we went on downstream. Dalton pointed to another rock, visible barely under the water's surface, but causing a white-foaming ripple. "There." He pointed. "That rock's just under the surface. See it?"

Kent nodded. "Um-m."

Dalton: "That's a dangerous rock to boatmen on this river."

"Why?"

"They could get hung up on it. Stranded. Upset. Rip the raft. Sink." He paused a moment, then looked at Kent Thomas. "Chala like that?"

A broad grin formed on Kent's face. "Dalton, you're beginning to get the idea."

We watched the river for a while—the eddies curling powerfully around, the currents forming vortices, bringing water to the surface in roiling masses, then pulling them under again.

Dalton continued. "I would go on, then, Kent, to guess that Chala's playing a dangerous game. So dangerous that he scares people. He's got a human tide against him."

Kent puffed on his pipe, saying nothing.

Dalton persisted. "What game? What people? I still don't understand."

At length Kent spoke slowly. In carefully crafted phrases. His eyes glazed. His thoughts far away. "Chala grew up in the jungle. He walked the trails, climbed the trees, came to know every leaf, every ant, everything that lived. He was a lot like other boys the world over. And yet, he developed, somehow, an out-of-the-ordinary passion for the natural world around him. His religion did not preach that animals were put on earth for him to use. Instead, they were his brothers. Snakes didn't frighten him. Spiders were to him just another part of the wonderful scheme of life."

"I can understand."

"And so he became rather famous among the villages. He had a gift of love for wild animals that went beyond what anyone had ever seen. He played with them, gave them names. Got to know their habits, how smart they were. Learned to respect them ... A kind of boy's love that never left him. In some respects, he's more a boy today than a man, enthusiastic, open-minded, compassionate."

Dalton said quietly: "We go with that around here. Respecting animals. Protecting them. We can relate."

Kent continued: "A lot of people can't. After they grow up, they put animals aside as just another phase of childhood and get to the business of making a living. Animals are simply relegated to minor status. But not with Chala ..."

Kent paused for a while, puffing on his pipe and surveying the cliffs above. Stubbs waited, curious now as to what would come of all this. He glanced at Chala, the cowboy hat turning in all directions, like that of a boy entering a new world... Then Kent went on.

"One day a cousin of his brought some white hunters to their village. Hunters who paid good money to get trophies ...

"The animals had never been harmed by Chala. So they trusted human beings. They trusted the hunters. Walked up to them. No fear. And then, the hunters shot a lot of these animals dead. Point blank range. Animals Chala had been playing with. Shot them and left some of them decapitated, some skinned, some rotting on the grass."

The passengers aboard the raft listened transfixed. I had heard it all in Nairobi. Their eyes scanned the cliffs and side canyons. Their minds tried to comprehend the range of emotions that must have filled the African boy's mind.

Kent Thomas continued. "The kid cried for days and weeks. He asked everybody he could find what the animals had done wrong that people wanted to hurt them. Put bullets in them. Cut off their heads. Rip away their skins. He asked why nobody had warned him these people were coming. Or even told him people like that existed. He couldn't believe it."

Cynthia spoke softly in a voice filled with disgust. "That's awful."

"The kid kept on crying for his lost friends. The villagers tried to comfort him, but they could do nothing. He went off and sat quietly alone, or with some of the animals that survived. He asked the animals why white men came. Why they had guns. Why they killed. He got no answers. No human told him. No animal could tell him. To this boy it was a thing incomprehensible."

Eddie Roff said: "That was a damned unusual kid ... This was in Africa?"

"Yes."

Cynthia mused: "I think I get it. He grew up determined to do something for the animals ... for all wildlife."

Kent went on. "He became known far and wide for this passion of his. It grew into an obsession. In the university he remained a kind of oddball, thinking more of animals than men. Preaching for the salvation of beasts instead of the salvation of man. The Muslims and Christians would have nothing to do with him."

Cynthia: "I see the problem"

Stubbs: "Some kind of nut."

Cynthia: "But if he was so impassioned, so on a single track, he couldn't be dismissed. Surely, people would pay some real attention to him."

Kent smiled slightly and looked at her with an understanding glance. "He got appointed to the United Nations Environment Programme. Moved to Nairobi. There he heard all this stuff about human rights. That every human being has a right to live in peace. In pursuit of happiness. Equal rights before God. Before *God*... It went to the seat of his brain like an arrow. His gods had said that everything was sacred. The ground. The grass. The trees. *Everything.* Man no more than grass. No more than animals..."

Cynthia mused. "We have some Indians around here who think that way. That the sun isn't put up in the sky just for us."

Kent nodded and looked down at the flowing river. "Someone brought to Chala an old Tibetan chant that said the writings of the wise ones were for man and beast. *Man and beast.* On an *equal* basis. Not man *over* beast. Not man *above* beasts. But man *alongside* beasts. *Equal* to them..."

Dalton Stubbs said: "Animal rights is an old idea. It's been around. What's Chala's angle"

Kent stopped, as though not sure whether to go on. Whether his listeners would understand fully the profound meaning of his next statement. When he spoke, his voice had a gentle air, almost casual, which emphasized the force and meaning of the sentence.

"He wants to make the rights of wild animals legal."

Cynthia Kasbolt whirled around on the pontoon and faced Kent squarely.

"Legal?" she asked, in a voice that said: *You can't mean it!*

"Legal," Kent responded. "Like lawful. Worldwide."

Dalton Stubbs issued a long, slow whistle. "I'm not sure I'm hearing right. Do you mean that if a man killed an animal, the man would be guilty of...of...*murder?*"

Kent responded. "The matter is too difficult for simple answers. Just as homicide is."

Stubbs: "But you're talking of man and animal equal before the law?"

Kent: "As is the case in other countries... As has been the case since ancient Egypt."

Stubbs: "Equal?"

Kent: "Yes. Animals have long been sacred. The Egyptians had animal gods. In times of famine, they would eat each other before they would eat a sacred animal. By contrast, Christians and others sacrificed animals on altars. Buddha thought the slaughtering of animals useless."

Cynthia: "Some people still do."

Kent: "A *lot* of people still do—in India, Nepal, China. It's an old idea that a man was clean and pure only if he had not eaten the flesh of animals, including fish. It was animals who first symbolized ideas, and that is engraved on the oldest monuments. Serpents were sacred to the Greeks and other early cultures. But then animals were slain mercilessly, brutally, in the *names* of the gods. It doesn't make any sense, really."

Cynthia: "My God, I agree. This is fascinating. Do go on."

"Animals came to be looked on as savage, horrid, brutes. Then came the Pythagoreans, who believed that human souls interchanged with other humans as well as animals."

Dalton: "You mean—well, that I shouldn't harm a deer because the creature might be my grandfather?"

"It's called *metempsychosis*, the transmigration of souls. A doctrine still held by natives of India."

For a few moments the only sounds came from the lapping of river waters against the pontoons of the raft. Eyes still searched the cliffs and shores, but brains fixed on Kent's every word.

"I don't know when, and perhaps there's no specific time or place, but human beings began to respect animals for their own sake. Fight to save them. Save their habitat. All that. Thomas Paine said in *The Age of Reason* that cruelty to animals is a violation of moral duty. Well, I could go on about Mozart and his starling, Robert Schumann, Oscar Wilde... But Chala wants to start in motion a procedure to give wild animals rights equal to those of man."

Cynthia slapped her forehead. "My God! Here in the American West? Does he know what he's doing? They're right! Chala's in trouble. The hunters will brand him a madman."

Kent: "They already have. And idiot. And moron. And subversive. A tyrant. You get the idea."

"I certainly do. And the idea is: he won't be alive much longer..."

The layered brown walls now surrounded the expedition, hemming it in, rising abruptly on each side of the river.

The three rafts floated gently under Navajo Bridge, a deck arch span with buttresses set on sandstone ledges. The Arizona Highway Patrol had stopped traffic on Highway 89A across the bridge until the three rafts had gone beneath. After that, the rangers remained on special alert, scanning every rim, every promontory, until the canyon widened again. The cross-bedded layers of the Coconino sandstone appeared...

The boatmen turned off motors. Again the rafts floated in all positions, sometimes sideways, sometimes stern first, borne on the currents of a wide and placid Colorado. The guides took care to steer away from boulders, fallen and submerged, that could snag the rafts.

Sam Petrie, in the third raft, snorted and tried to adjust his floppy, broad-brimmed hat.

"I hate hats!" So saying, he took it off.

I pointed skyward. "Sun's still up there, Sam. Haze or no haze. You want your sexy bald pate sizzled?"

Sam's bald top glistened in the bright light. He tried to arrange the last remnants of hair around his ears. Snorting again, he gave up and put the hat back on.

I scanned the river, keeping my eyes on a yellow raft far behind but gaining on us.

"Do you realize, Sam?" I said. "You've sent me on dozens of assignments around the world, but this is the first time you've ever come along yourself?"

"First time I ever sent you down the Colorado River, m'lad. I'm still a boy, Barry. I've always wanted to raft down this river."

"Could be dangerous..."

"Bravo! That's the best part of it. Bad as New York, you think?"

I shrugged. Sam went on. "Barry, you're the foremost person in the world to know what danger is. God, you've been a help to us. You've solved cases we would never have—."

I interrupted. "Thank Aunt Kelly. She wants this planet cleaned up and we're not doing it fast enough."

Sam cast a playful glance my way. "You're the only rich playboy I know who's trying to save the world instead of wreck it."

I raised an eyebrow. "Have to do something with her millions. She likes you, Sam. Did you know that?"

"She's sweet. We like her, too. And her millions..."

I watched the yellow raft drawing closer. "Tell me," he said, "you think Chala has a chance?"

I shrugged my shoulders. "He's placing his first proposal before the Council when he gets back. Very modest. Legal rights for tigers. That's all. Nothing more."

Sam asked: "How's it stated?"

"Same as I drafted it for him. That tigers have as much right to exist on this planet as human beings, and no statute, no moral law, no scripture gives us the right to wipe them out. Reasonable? Not too far out?"

Sam looked puzzled. "Easy to say, Barry. You're on the tiger's side. But you should have seen the shit fly when word of this first got out."

"Oh, come on, Sam, people have been plugging for animal rights for years—rats in research labs, monkeys in hospitals—everybody knows that."

"Yeah, I know, but this is not about laboratory animals. Or food stocks like cattle and chickens. This is native animals in their wild habitats. The things people hunt."

"Go on."

"Well, nobody this high in a world agency has tried to put it into a *legal* code. To make it *binding*. Chala really hit the fan on this one."

I scoffed. "Oh, hell, Sam. We're only talking about tigers. They're disappearing..."

"Sure. But we get hit by environment buffs who think we should put *all* endangered wildlife in the proposal."

"So?"

"Then we get hit by hunters. They're saying deer will be next. Every angler is saying fish will be next. The fur trade is scared to death by this. They're screaming. *'You'll make us murderers! All of us! We'll be run out of business!'*"

"Sam, they're only scared because the public is beginning to get behind this..."

"Not very many, Barry ..."

"Enough to scare people."

"Okay."

Dee Dunn, one of Sam Petrie's colleagues at the United Nations in New York, had listened carefully, smiling and nodding from time to time. Now she spoke. "The British are beginning to rise up against fox hunting. Can you believe that? The polls say so. A tradition. Centuries old. This sentiment in favor of wild animals is rising faster than we may think. It's real."

Mozo Fernandez said: "Sounds to me like the guy is either a psycho or a dreamer."

Buck Stevens: "Or he's just a century ahead of his time."

Dee Dunn: "That question intrigued me, and I asked Chala if I couldn't look into it, to see if there was a ghost of a chance of *any* proposal succeeding."

Buck: "Well, of course, there's a lot of flak against using live animals for medical experiments..."

Dee: "I knew that. It's part of the support we have. But I wanted to go beyond that. And what I found so encouraged Chala that he advanced his timetable."

Mozo: "Why? What did you find."

Dee: "Well, for one thing, I knew that Buddhism and Hinduism are very strong on animal appreciation—not to mention the ancient Egyptians and American Indians and so on. I wanted to see if so powerful a religion as Christianity had anything to offer. On a trip to Oaxaca, Mexico, last August I attended an annual ceremony called 'The Blessing of the Animals,' in which people dressed up dogs, cats, pigs, rabbits, a horse and other animals, and took them to the church, where the animals received a blessing. Now I'm trying to find out how widespread this is."

Buck: "You must have had a good laugh, at least."

Dee: "Yes, I did laugh. Then I remembered that this is the same religion that says 'the meek will inherit the earth.' "

Mozo: "I'm not impressed. That's not government policy."

Dee: "About that time, we got the results of a Gallup poll of twenty-two thousand people in twenty-two nations. Most respondents said they would give top priority to protecting the environment, even if it meant slowing economic growth. Right after that came a report from China that two farmers had been caught poaching pandas in one of the remote provinces."

"What happened?"

"They were executed."

"Executed? You really mean it? Both of them?"

"Yes."

"Now I'm impressed."

Dee went on. "I then went into the issue of national parks. Americans invented the idea of national parks, as you no doubt know. Oh, there had been royal reserves for years, sometimes opened to a monarch's subjects, but they were basically hunting reserves. The world's first people's park, as such, or national park, as it came to be known later, was Yellowstone. And those pioneers adopted the policy that these big natural areas would be places where human beings became the intruders. Intruders—that was a novel idea then. It had never been done before."

Mozo: "I see what you're driving at. Chala's is today's novel idea."

"You catch on fast."

"Then—so what?"

"So I found that this idea has grown terrifically. Today there are thousands of nature reserves, including national parks, in more than a hundred countries. Some countries have, you might say, exploded with national parks, just in the last few years. Costa Rica is the best example. And now tourism to these places is booming. It's a heritage thing, then an economic thing. What Chala is saying, basically, is—kill the tigers and you not only wipe out a species, but you kill a lot of tourism. The bottom line, gentlemen, is that Chala's life is threatened just for *proposing* legal rights for animals..."

My eyes, still on the approaching yellow raft, almost within rifle range, narrowed. "Dee, we have had people killed for proposing a lot less."

"Such as?"

"Well, an Audubon warden named Guy Bradley, for one. He tried to save the herons and egrets of southern Florida from being exterminated by plume hunters."

"Plume hunters?" she asked.

"Plumes on ladies' hats. All the rage at the turn of the century. Big money. So one day they found warden Bradley in a pool of blood in his canoe...out in the mangroves of the coastal Everglades."

Dee recoiled. "Ugh! Well, the hunters finally lost on *that* one. Plumes are not used now."

I said: "They will lose on this one, too...some day. They know that. That's the problem. They want to stop it. They want to stop Chala. Now. They don't even want this thing *mentioned.*"

Dee lowered her head. "That's why Chala's in danger."

The yellow boat had come within range.

I signaled to Rudy Vogel to start the engine.

We joined the other rafts, which at that moment floated along the opposite bank. Rudy turned off the motor.

We stayed there, all three rafts more or less together, drifting past fallen sandstone blocks and, on shore, copses of mesquite. Joe and the rangers took up their rifles.

The yellow raft held its course along the left bank.

Rudy scanned it with his binoculars. "Looks okay to me. Boatman's a friend o' mine. That's Mike Faddis with what looks like a family of six."

We settled back into what passed for relaxation, resuming our all-points watch.

Mozo Fernandez, the ranger from Coronado National Memorial, had overheard part of the exchange among Sam, Dee and me. A trace of anxiety had appeared on his face. He leaned over to me and asked quietly: "*Are* deer going to be next?"

Sam leaned back and looked up. Assassins hid on every ledge, popped up on every rim. "The heat's getting to me," he thought. He looked farther up, saw where the mammoth boulders in the river had come—from sheer walls from which whole cliff faces had broken off and thundered down. Cornices and ledges that looked as though they'd been freshly sheared—yesterday? A thousand years ago? A million? Rocks as large as houses rested on the river bank. He shuddered to imagine the crash and commotion when they fell.

"Remind me, Barry," he said, "not to sleep under a cliff tonight."

"It's all right, Sam," I kidded him, "you'll be in a tent."

Sam pulled a trailing blue bag from the water and took out a beer. Opening it, he said: "Here's to—."

Without warning, the boatmen started their motors.

"Badger Creek Rapids," Rudy shouted. "Fifteen foot drop. Class five. Take your places."

I looked for campsites along the river, or boats hidden among the shrubbery.

We left the pontoons and took seats on the deck. Following instructions, we grasped the cargo ropes, faced outward, and held tightly. Sam clung to the beer between his knees.

I checked the walls. Every ledge. Every overhang. Every hidden crevice. Every shadow.

In the first raft, Joe Muck watched with intense fascination as the river's peaceful green turned to agitated white and broke into choppy waves at the edge of the rapid. Violent floods over the centuries past had hurled huge boulders from side streams out into the main river, partially blocking it. These disrupted the flow of the Colorado, converting the surface into a mass of curling, rolling, leaping white fountains. Churning waters stretched from one canyon wall to the other.

Just as we went off, I checked every boulder on both sides. No one hiding...but I couldn't be sure.

The water's last glistening smoothness lay like a long green tongue at the lip of the fall. Approaching this, each boatmen steered his raft to avoid any hidden boulders, trying to keep it from getting skewed around or hung up. If they accidentally started down the rapid sideways, they could get into trouble. Or if they started on the wrong trajectory one that could throw them against a pile of boulders or a very unyielding cliff—we could capsize.

The raft edged closer to the "jump-off" point. Joe shouted: "Here we go!"

He saw the powerful force of the current driving water over the edge in a surging torrent.

Off went the raft. The front end dropped with a loud *thump!* The vessel skewed, turned sideways. Water struck the pontoons, shooting spray into the air and raining icy water down on the passengers.

"Ai-yee-ee!" Joe Muck shouted in his typical cowboy fashion. "That's *cold!* Let's *git* 'em!"

The raft jerked and bumped as though descending stairs, and before we knew it, rushed out onto a placid water surface below.

"Aw, Rudy," Joe yelled, "that wasn't very much!"

"Jest you wait, cowboy!" Rudy called forward. "Jest you wait!"

"Wait for what?"

"That's only a Class Five rapid. Wait'll you git to Class Ten."

"When's that?"

"Day after tomorrow."

Joe watched the water, riffles, and rapids as the miles passed, mesmerized by the river's power. We came out from behind a pile of rocks, from which we could have been fired upon from behind. I almost wrenched my back from twisting and turning so fast against the pontoon.

Before long, the water erupted anew. Giant floods of the past had rolled another mass of boulders from a side canyon and strewn them across the Colorado, this time almost damming it. Only at the far edge could the mighty river get through.

This partial dam forced the surging currents leftward on a sweeping double curve into a narrow channel of torrential waves. The white water crashed and tumbled against the red Supai sandstones and shales. To navigate this chute, each boatman had to maneuver his raft as best he could—to the proper position for entry. Once we left the lip, we'd be at the river's mercy.

Rudy shouted: "Hang on for this one!"

I did another sweeping scan of all the new ledges and crevices.

Away we went! Over the edge. Down with a thump. Covered with a flying sheet of frigid spray.

The surging current gripped the raft and flung it to the right. Another torrent lifted it, tilted it, and hurled it to the left. The waters aimed the raft directly toward the opposite wall. The surge then bore it on a long curve to the right, down the roaring chute. The raft heaved and twisted, almost grazing the sandstone walls. Spray flew again and again. Water filled the air, struck our faces with sharp slaps.

We clung to the ropes as the vessel lurched, trying to dodge the spray. We turned our heads—only to take full in the face an unexpected blast of frigid water from another angle. For all the punishment, everyone shrieked and howled and roared with glee.

"Ai-yeee!" Joe shouted again.

"Ow-wooo!" Chala howled amid the general chorus.

Joe exulted. The African champion of wildlife—having the time of his life in a deep canyon thousands of miles from his homeland. What a contrast! Yet, how satisfying the love of the wild, Joe thought, crossing all racial and cultural boundaries. For Chala, it would be the greatest time of his life.

I was pleased that we were swerving right and left, targets hard to zero in on.

The water kept churning for some distance along the river, erupting with whitecaps. When all calmed down at last, the rafts eased out onto smooth water. The passengers stood, stretched, and toweled away what water they could.

"No extra charge for the shower!" Joe called.

After this, the distant canyon walls seemed to grow higher, towering more than a thousand feet above the river. I relaxed. At least an assassin on *those* cliffs would be too high and too far back to reach the rafts with a bullet.

But now we were slower targets. Anyone with telescopic sights would have time to aim...pull the trigger...squeeze...

The overcast of haze began to dissipate. The sky changed to deep blue. The heat became intense, ameliorated only by cooling breezes above the water surface. Passengers and boatmen, floppy hats pulled low, dark glasses hiding their eyes, took on an aspect of wide-eyed aliens from distant space.

After a while the boatmen steered toward a sand bank, stopped, and tied up the rafts.

"Indian ruins!" called Jerry Elliott.

The rangers disembarked first, setting themselves up at security positions.

The passengers clambered over the pontoons and went ashore. We started up a trail along a talus slope of broken rocks, tricky to navigate, to view the remnants of prehistoric Indian structures.

Julie joined Joe Muck. "Barry's been telling me some amazing things about you."

Joe nodded and smiled. "He tries to be modest."

"How'd he get into all this?"

"Well, he's a wildlife graduate. Got into law enforcement. Then worldwide environmental law. Been everywhere. Uncanny sense of human nature."

"That's what he said about you."

"Recognizes real talent. We have lots of cases."

"Cases? You mean murder cases?"

"Mostly."

"Then you're always looking for clues."

"We don't look much for clues. We let the police do that."

Julie seemed incredulous. "You don't look for clues? How else can you track down people?"

"Human nature. We go after the logic of human actions and reactions."

"Barry does this?"

"He won't take on anything except world stuff, big stuff. Sam Petrie got on to him years ago, saw his talents, began asking him to help out on UN programs. Mostly stuff too dangerous or delicate for others to handle."

"He's employed by the UN?"

"No. Independent."

"Rich? If you don't mind my asking?"

"His Aunt Kelly. She funds everything. Wanted to put her millions where they'd count. Cleaning up the mess people have made on earth. Tracking criminals, poachers, pushing laws. Kind of a personal crusade with her."

Julie's eyes seemed to widen with each step of this inquiry. "Barry said you met him in the Amazon."

"That was some trip."

"And he took you with him to Mount Everest?"

"That was a little hairy."

"Then he sent you to school in Paris?"

"Well, Aunt Kelly did."

"Terrific. She must like you."

"Anyone Barry likes, she likes."

"So you're here."

"And having one helluva good time, I'll tell you that!"

They climbed carefully, their footing among the rocks tricky. She pointed out the sparse vegetation: cactus among the rocks, yucca, Mormon tea, clumps of tall grass. "Whatever grows down here," she said, "has to be able to survive temperatures of a hundred and eighty degrees next to the ground."

He looked at her. "How do *you* survive?"

She laughed. "I stay in the shade. It's only a hundred and twenty there."

"How do lizards live?"

She answered with a smile. "They stay in the shade, too."

"Logical, huh? Rattlesnakes?"

"Same."

"You ever see any?"

"Here and there."

"You sound almost casual."

"I *like* rattlers. Wonderfully adapted to these rocks. Good defense mechanisms. Poison very effective. Nature did an efficient job when she built the rattlesnake."

"He."

They laughed, climbed to the ruins, talked about the long history of man in the canyon. Angel Ingebretson, the park historian, joined our little group, elaborating on how human beings lived here, struggled to explore the river, and

eventually "fought like hell," she said, "to keep the Grand Canyon the way it is."

"When did the Indians arrive here?" Joe asked.

"Some time between three thousand and five thousand years ago," Angel answered, "as near as we can tell. We find stick figures in caves in the Redwall limestone. These early people were probably hunters. Then came farmers, then the Basketmakers. They often lived in caves and tilled what earth they could find in these canyons. Then came the Pueblo Indians. We find all kinds of debris—pieces of pottery, prayer sticks, pipes and the like—that tells a lot about them."

"How many people?" Dee asked.

"Well, five hundred pueblo ruins have been found in the canyon, most of them relatively small."

"Any descendants?"

"Yes, but not here. The canyon dwellers left about eight hundred years ago."

"Why?"

"We're not sure. Enemies, perhaps. Drought. Or a variety of reasons. The Havasupai, now living in the western end of the Grand Canyon, are a Yuman-speaking people, and they've occupied their canyon for at least eight hundred years."

As we turned to leave, Joe said: "This canyon has been busier than I thought."

By the time we got back to the rafts, the sun's heat had become more intense. Joe peeled to his swim suit and dived into the pool beside the rafts. Shrieking, he dived right out again. "Ai-yee-ee! What a contrast between air and water!"

Julie laughed. "I heard you sizzling when you went in!"

We passed Vasey's Paradise, where springs poured out and fell over steps of stone into a patch of dark green vegetation below. We skirted the far side of the channel and did not stop, for tourists clambered over the slopes. I judged the risk too great.

Buck Stevens wore a puzzled look.

I asked: "Something's bothering you."

"Frankly, yes," Buck replied. "So Chala wants to save the tiger. I don't see how he can do it. There are so many poor and hungry people in Asia. Millions. And he's only one man."

Sam Petrie spoke up. "I used to think the whole thing was hopeless myself. But, I just got some new perspective."

"Be serious now."

"I am. Last month I got back from Patagonia, down in Argentina. They've brought back the sea elephant. Colonies of sea lions. And the Magellanic penguins—by God, ships used to land and the sailors would kill twenty thousand penguins

a day, just for the sport of it. When those birds are nesting they stay on their eggs no matter what. The gunners could just walk up to them. Pow! That was it.

"Now the Argentines have set up reserves. Staffed them with young and eager patriots, biologists. Birds nest by the millions in Chubut Province. In March, at the end of the breeding season, the penguins gather on the shores. You should see it! Then they all go to sea. Nobody knows where. Don't tell me there aren't mysteries left in this world! Anyway—I learned not to give up. Maybe we can do the same with tigers. We *have* to."

Buck said: "Hard to believe, Sam."

"Damn right. I looked at all those penguins with my two eyes and still couldn't believe it. It was incredible."

Buck: "I'd like to see that, Sam."

Sam: "Buck, if you get Chala through this canyon alive, I'll see that you get to Patagonia."

I interrupted: "You mean you'll ask Aunt Kelly if she'll send him down there."

Sam: "Of course. Maybe we'd better send her an Indian rug or something while we're out this way, Barry, huh?"

"And charge it to her account as expenses?"

"Barry, your brain is full of larceny."

"Sam, it's your brain has the larceny. I merely detected it."

"Promise you won't tell?"

"For Buck's sake? I'm as silent as that chunk of sandstone over there."

The inner canyon narrowed further, the river coursing between sheer cliffs of Redwall limestone. Here, however, the "Redwall" had not a trace of red. In other places it wore a coating of sediments washed by rain from the dark red Supai formation above This far down into the canyon, the massive cliffs showed their solid, gray, natural make-up.

Such a durable rock could support vast caverns.

And now we came to one.

At one bend, the relentless flow of sand and gravel in the Colorado River had scoured out a long cavern with a low roof, as though someone had gouged out a layer cake at the bottom.

"Redwall Cavern ahead," Rudy announced. "Time to chow up."

Joe Muck, in the front raft, surveyed the dories, rafts and canoes tied up. And the tourists in the cavern, playing volley ball. No danger apparent. He gave a signal to proceed with landing.

I went on yellow alert. "Risky," I thought. "I hope we have enough people to manage any surprise."

The rangers spread out over the sandy floor of the cave, which would hold 50,000 people, Rudy said, "if you c'd git that many together peacefully."

After the park staff had sealed off a corner of the cavern, the passengers dismounted—Chala flanked by bodyguards. Boat crews brought food chests up from the rafts and the passengers fell to making sandwiches.

Well, all except Chala, who sent on the bodyguards and stayed behind, committing the ranger's nightmare. Accompanied only by Tip Phrakonekham and Dietrich Deitemeyer, he went down to the shore and began conversing with other travelers.

Joe watched from a rock above the river, where he sat with Julie. "I give up!"

"Don't worry," Julie said. "VIPs always like to mingle. They know the risks."

Joe surveyed the rafts, rowboats, dories, kayaks and inflated canoes tied up to the rocks. "What's the river flow?" he asked.

"It can get up near a hundred thousand cubic feet per second," she replied.

"Ai-yee-ee! Don't some of those dinky things capsize in the big rapids?"

"Sure," she answered. "Everything upsets sooner or later. Happens all the time."

"Will we?"

"Maybe."

"How deep is the river?"

"Hundred feet in some places."

"Don't people get drowned?"

"Sure."

"Well, this is a dangerous river."

She glanced at him with an air of helplessness and nodded toward the canoes and kayaks. "You tell them that."

"Can't you stop it?"

"We don't want to remove all danger from the river."

"But you're the ones who have to pull out the bodies."

"We regulate this use. We only permit two dozen or so outfitters to take people down the canyon."

"Can people go on their own?"

"Yes. About a third of river use is private. They have to wait years sometimes for a permit. We have to control use down here or too many people would love the canyon to death. Trample the vegetation. Foul up the streams. This is a fragile desert. We have nearly forty thousand people backpacking into the canyon each year on overnight permits. We think that's all the canyon can take."

"Don't you spread 'em out?"

"There are sixteen trails into the canyon, most of them primitive. We don't maintain those. We don't fix them up. They're not safe. A tough go."

"What happens?"

"Oh, people slip on rocks and fall. They get lost when landslides obliterate sections of trail. Their biggest problem is heat. Temperatures over a hundred degrees daily in summer. Hikers have to carry canteens with them and water's *heavy*. They don't carry enough. We recommend a gallon of water a day per person. Otherwise, dehydration sets in, then heat exhaustion, fatigue, vomiting, nausea, fainting—the works. Or people will rely on springs they see marked on a map, but there's no water there any more. In winter, they suffer from hypothermia. Never a dull minute..."

Joe munched his sandwich and remained thoughtful for a few moments. Then he said: "I've told you all about me. What about you? Why are *you* here?"

"Just a minute," Julie said. "There's one more thing you haven't told me."

"What?"

"There's no one with you."

"I'm at work. With Barry on assignment."

"You beg my question."

Joe grinned. "You're persistent. I like that in a person."

"So—?"

"All right. She's at the shopping mall in Laramie."

"Shopping?"

"I hope so."

"What do you mean by that?"

Joe grinned widely at her question. "That's where she *said* she'd be. Never mind. She's not the river type. Now, what about you?"

"Okay," Julie answered. "I teach at the University of Kentucky. Geology department."

"There's no one with you," he mocked.

"No," she answered simply. Then she smiled. "I don't have anyone shopping in the mall."

They watched Chala and his entourage come back up the sandy slope to have their lunch.

Joe scanned the other river runners. No guns. No threats. Nothing suspicious...yet.

Julie, Woody Watkins and I watched Joe and the rangers playing volley ball.

Woody said, lighting a pipe: "Joe would make a good ranger here."

I responded: "Joe would make a good ranger anywhere."

"What does he think about this project?"

"He's pretty dedicated. He thinks Chala is on to something."

"Is he?"

Before I could answer, a shout came from behind us.

"Dr. Ross. A catastrophe!"

We turned to see Margie Cox, the cook, running across the sandy slope toward them. "A catastrophe!" she repeated.

I caught her by the arm. "Margie, what happened?"

"It's the lunch, Dr. Ross. The lunch meats—all we have are ham and pork. Chala doesn't eat ham or pork. It's a disaster. What'll we do? Deitemeyer's furious!"

I frowned: "I told them to plan for this."

Margie: "Nobody told me about it."

"Okay, where's your reserve food box?"

"At the raft."

I took her hand. "Come with me."

We ran to the raft, rummaged through some boxes, took out a couple of items, and climbed back up through the soft sand to the lunch table.

Deitemeyer met us head-on. "Barry—! I thought I made clear exactly what diet we were to follow. What's the meaning of this?"

"Now, Dietrich—."

"It's an insult to His Eminence! I don't know how we'll get out of this one. He's hungry."

I spied Chala, standing near the back of the cave, and strolled over nonchalantly. "Ah, Mon Eminence!"

"Barry, mon ami," Chala said, clasping me as I came up. Margie Cox stood a pace behind.

I spoke rapidly. "Mon Eminence, je vous prie ... Ce repas delectable nous avons preparé especialement pour un maître de la rivière."

Chala rocked with laughter. He gloried in being called "master of the river." But a special lunch? For him? Curiosity overwhelmed him.

"Pour moi?" he asked, twiddling his fingers with anticipation. "Qu'est-ce que nous avons ici?"

I answered: "Quelque chose pour un gourmand."

I treated the two small cans as though they held delights for a princely feast.

He held one up. "Les noix chinoises," he said, fumbling for a French version of Chinese water chestnuts.

Chala beamed. "Pour moi? Barry! Ma favorite!"

I held up the other can, containing chunks of turkey meat, and said, with a flourish: "Des morceaux de dinde!"

Chala smacked his lips, took the can, and held it up like a shaman holding aloft an offering to the gods. "Pieces de resistance! Barry, vous êtes un maître de la rivière."

Chala howled at his own reference to me as a master chef of the river. I motioned Margie to take over, suggested she serve the contents of the two cans on a bed of lettuce, then withdrew, with a salute to Chala.

When I got back to Julie and Woody, they listened entranced to the episode of water chestnuts and turkey chunks.

"Barry," said Julie, "I wish I had a tenth of your diplomatic skills."

"Human nature," I answered.

She said, surprised: "That's the same term Joe used."

I turned to Woody. "You were asking whether Chala is really onto something."

"Yes."

I paused before replying. "I think so. Ahead of his time, perhaps, but yes, I think he's on a valid crusade."

Woody: "Sounds a bit Quixotic. He's going to have a tough time, Barry."

"Chala knows that. What do you think?"

"Me? Oh, I pay no attention. I can't take sides."

"You don't hunt?"

"Not me. We in the public service have to remain neutral."

"That must be a tough go."

"Not really."

I frowned. "Your job is protecting wildlife. I'd think you'd embrace Chala's ideas."

Woody shrugged without comment.

I went on: "What if Chala prevails? That bother you any?"

Woody remained thoughtful for a moment. "I'd think of it for the most part as a massive law enforcement problem. As for us, we have a population control program on feral burros in the park. If I had to stop that...stop removing burros..."

I finished the sentence. "They'd multiply."

Woody looked at me with a serious countenance. "Maybe Chala could put exceptions into his proposal?"

"Maybe," I answered. "He's pretty single minded, though. He's got an African focus."

"You helping him?"

"I helped him draft the proposal."

Woody looked down at the sand. "You think it's doomed?"

"Most political proposals are, at first."

"But you'll keep at it?"

I turned noncommittal. "Why not?"

"And Chala? Is he unstoppable?"

I smiled and nodded. "Definitely."

For a while after leaving Redwall Cavern, the raft crew paused and exchanged information with other crews they met. Word had gotten out about the VIP on the river, and it bothered me to have so many rafts and rowboats so near.

As the Chala raft neared each dory, Joe Muck, in the first raft, scanned the passengers, looked for signs of hostility, and placed his rifle beside him. For the most part, however, the river guides did as they always had: exchanged beer or cigarettes, sized up the camping spots ahead, and passed on scuttlebutt about other river runners.

The passengers in the boats we met appeared to be mostly families. Sometimes the retinue included the family dog. In smaller, crowded rafts, passengers sat atop the stowage. I noted that every duffel bag, every box, and every piece of equipment had been waterproofed and tied down. "For the times," I thought, "when the raft would go completely under water."

It only reminded me of the violent nature of this river, and the crashing, massive rapids we had yet to see... The ones when even *we*, in the big rafts, would go under.

The passengers, learning by a kind of river grapevine communication, had heard only of the "VIP from Africa. Some kind of prince." When they saw him—that black face under the cowboy hat—they waved and cheered. Typical, warmhearted American greeting, Neff Neilson assured Chala. The African prince then took off his cowboy hat and waved back.

Eventually, the traffic thinned. For a while we floated lazily, entering placid pools where the guides let the rafts go free, slowly turning. We stared at soaring red walls far above, then at the drifting white clouds, each tinted pink on the underside, a reflection of the rich red landscapes underneath.

As the canyons became narrower, Chala's cowboy hat fell off every time he looked up, whereupon he hurled it into a corner of the raft and tried to forget about it. Tip put it on and wore it to protect it.

Mesmerized by the slowly rotating scenes, we fell into a lethargy. A few slept, but Joe, the rangers and I kept a lookout for any movement ahead, from the river banks up the walls to the rims of nearby cliffs.

Sometimes the gentle passage made us feel as though we drifted in a dream. The walls became diaphanous curtains of red and pink and brown, gateways that eased us to some celestial paradise. Cupped in the rafts, heads back on pontoons or cargo, everyone fought to stay awake, to glimpse the passing walls and crags...

Kent Thomas said to Cynthia Kasbolt: "What I would give to hear a ninety-voice choir sing a Bach Chorale Prelude in one of those amphitheaters. Nothing more. Just that. Then I could die in peace."

"That's funny," she responded. "I was thinking more or less the same thing. All these amphitheaters with no orchestra. No music. No chorus. Just murderers."

Suddenly, Woody Watkins went rigid. He spoke quietly to alert Joe and the rangers aboard. "Something moving on the slope ahead. On the right. Two o'clock."

Sunglasses came off. Binoculars went up. Guns came out.

Into his microphone Watkins said: "B.J. We have something moving ahead. Right wall. Talus slope. Get Chala covered.

Joe got his rifle out and ready. He squinted and scanned the slope, but saw nothing.

On the third raft, I heard Woody's warning on Buck Stevens's radio. I sat up and scanned the cliff with binoculars. No movement. Nothing.

B.J. Pritchett came on the air in a moment. "Uh...we don't see from here, Woody. Can you repeat?"

From Woody: "Find the cliff up there, go down to the big house-size blocks fallen just below it. Right in there."

Pritchett: "We're looking."

On my signal, motors came to life and the rafts moved rapidly down the river on the left. "Case anyone wants to roll rocks down on us," I said to Buck.

After another minute, I said, "Still don't see anything."

Buck answered: "I do."

I took my eyes away from my binoculars and looked over at Buck Stevens, who sat with his head down, grinning from ear to ear.

I asked: "What is the matter with you?"

Buck did not answer at once. He called Sam, Julie, Dee, Mozo, Kathi and me into a huddle, pointing at the cluster of rocks above.

"Two bighorn bucks. In the shadows. Base of that big rock. See 'em?"

They gasped. I said: "Then why don't you inform Woody?"

"I'm to inform the Assistant Superintendent of this park that he mistook some bighorn sheep for killers and alerted all three rafts for nothing?"

I smiled. "You are one astute politician, Buck. Mind if I do it?"

Buck handed over the microphone and I spoke into it. "Woody? Barry. I think you got two bighorns in the shadows up there. Suggest we return a little back up river and give Chala a good look."

Woody responded: "Thanks, Barry. We will."

Buck still grinned as the rafts returned up the placid pool for a better view. The boatmen turned off the motors.

Kathi LeClair asked: "How do they live up there? What do they eat? What do they drink?"

Buck answered, "You see some grass up there. We got lots of seeps in this canyon, places where water oozes out. Springs. That's where more grasses grow. Or these sheep can go to any side stream, pick up water and grasses year round."

Kathi: "But the canyon's so dry."

"Just looks dry. Most of the springs and grass are hidden up the side streams. Side canyons."

Dee Dunn could not imagine how any living animal kept its footing on such perilous cliffs and slopes. "Now don't tell us they never fall?"

"Well," Buck answered, "Mother Nature's not exactly what you'd call perfect. And anyway, if a bighorn gets old and can't climb very well, then one day it falls."

I added: "Their hooves make them pretty sure-footed up there."

Kathi asked: "What other mammals have you in the canyon? Mountain lions?"

"Yes. Uncommon, but here."

"Coyotes?"

"Yes."

"Foxes?"

"On the rims."

"Bobcats?"

"Common."

"Lots of deer, I know that. Beaver?"

"Not many."

"Lots of smaller animals?"

"Lots. Squirrels, jackrabbits, chipmunks, rats, mice. Birds. This is a busy place."

Kathi sighed. "You don't know what a breath of fresh air this conversation is to me."

"Why?

"Well, I'm getting tired of writing stories on how man has screwed up wild life." She nodded in the direction of Chala's raft. "Some day he's going to win."

The boats floated lazily down the river. The bighorns lay dozing in the shade of the fallen boulder.

The sun dropped behind the canyon rim early. After a few more rapids and riffles, with consequent wetting and drying, we rounded Point Hansbrough in a wide meander of the river, and approached the mouth of Saddle Canyon.

Here, the river had laid down a long flat sandy beach. The boatmen steered to the south end and tied up on shore. The passengers disembarked, formed a line, passed the baggage from one to another, and in a few minutes emptied the cargo.

Each then picked up his or her gear and walked up over a small dune and through a thicket of seepwillow to put up their tents.

Joe asked Ted Quail, the trip leader, a red-haired, red-faced man of bulk and brawn: "We need tents? It's too hot!"

Quail shrugged as he coiled a rope. "Do as you please. Sleep out on the sand."

"Expect any rain?"

"Could be. This is July. Sand's your worst problem."

"Sand? How come?"

"If a breeze comes up during the night, you'll have sand in your ears, eyes, nose..."

"Never mind," Joe said. "I'll put up a tent."

Joe and I helped locate a site and set up tents for Chala and his party, finding sites as safe and comfortable as possible for Sam Petrie, Dee Dunn, Tip Phrakonekham, Dietrich Deitemeyer, Kent Thomas and the bodyguards. These secluded campsites, each more or less screened by vegetation, lay beneath a rock wall that formed the outer edge of camp.

Chala and Joe sat for a long time on safari chairs, watching the sun leave one wall after another, bathing the cliffs with increasingly darker tints of orange and purple. Their conversation flowed from wildlife to parks to public use without hunting.

After that, as the long twilight began, Joe and I took a walk to examine the river shore.

I observed: "Not likely anyone would approach this camp by water."

Joe added: "Doesn't matter much. Both ends of camp are vulnerable."

"The rangers will have guards out. That's why we brought so many rangers. Round-the-clock surveillance."

Joe pointed to a distant lantern up river. "Any problem from over there?"

I shook my head. "Buck investigated. Small camp of tourists. He talked to them."

Joe remained edgy. "What about someone hidden? Came down the river ahead of us? Knew we'd camp here probably..."

"How would they know that?"

"Obvious. I didn't see many beaches big enough for three rafts and this many people. They could have landed and gone up the canyon till dark..."

"Anything's possible."

Joe pointed to the cliff above camp. "And what about up there. If they rolled some rocks down..." His voiced trailed off.

I nodded: "I scanned that cliff before we landed, Joe. Talked with Buck about it. The top doesn't seem accessible."

"Okay," Joe spread his hands. "We've done about all we can. Now we wait."

I changed the subject. "You talked with Chala. How's he doing?"

"This trip means more to him than just about anything. Such a big park. All this wildlife being protected. It's like an unbelievable dream to him... 'Rêve incroyable,' he called it. Gives him new vigor to go on with his wild animal project."

"You mean tiger crusade? He expects to win?"

"Nobody believes that. He knows it. He wonders sometimes: why not go for the gold? Codify all threatened animals at the outset. But then he sinks back and says it's too much for the human race to chew right now. He's a pioneer. Sometimes he has a feeling that time is running out. That he won't get enough species protected before they become extinct."

"Most pioneers fail...the first time out. I told him that. He has to keep at it...not get discouraged.

"He's not! Far from it. Just impatient. I sat with him a while, just now. He said: 'Animals are dying! Whole populations of tuna and whales and tigers are being wiped out. Nobody gave us authority to kill them. We took it! We just took it! We must stop it. Kill men if we must! But stop it!...' He really gets wound up."

Completing our perimeter patrol, we sauntered over to the ranger group, drawn by the teasing odors of sizzling steaks on a gas grill. No one lit a fire. No wood. No need for warmth with the temperature still at a hundred degrees.

"How are we going to get to sleep at this temperature?" asked Cynthia Kasbolt, accustomed to the cool, high mountain

breezes at Bryce Canyon National Park in Utah. "Buck, when does it cool off?"

"About three in the morning."

She recoiled. "Three?"

"Well, the rocks have been soaking up heat all day..."

"And they let it out all night... Okay. But I'm not going to sleep very much."

Buck had a solution. "Take a towel down to the river. Dip it and wring it out. Take it back to your sack and put it over you. The towel will have a temperature near forty-nine degrees."

Cynthia demurred. "Thanks, Buck. I don't want to freeze, either."

"I'm game," said Woody Watkins. "Sounds logical, if you want some sleep."

Neff Neilson, the park interpreter, joined the group. "I'm a nervous wreck."

Neff and Angel Ingebretson had been on Chala's raft all day. I sympathized. "How did you get along?"

Neff, a gentle "jack of all sciences," he called himself, sat with his head against a food box, and lanky legs propped up in front of him. For all the world he could have been an amiable farm lad, talking enthusiastically about lambs and crops and headers. But the precision of his words, his elegant phrases, his skills of explaining and simplifying, marked him a cultured man, able to make understandable anything about this canyon.

"Chala's a real treasure," he said, softly, "one of the greatest human beings I've ever met. Angel, I think, will go along..."

Angel Ingebretson, the park historian, sat beside him, hat off, her short cropped black hair suggesting an air of authority, logic, curiosity. "He's like I imagine some of the great figures in history," she said. "Larger than life. And yet, simple. Terrific thinker..."

Woody: "What sort of things did he ask about?"

Neff replied: "Well, the canyon, of course. The geology. Sometimes it took a while getting things first to Tip, who translated, and then to Chala. He wanted to know absolutely *everything* about this canyon. We saw a desert plume sending up its bright yellow spikes of flowers. The common name meant nothing. I said *Stanleya pinnata.* The scientific name didn't mean anything, either, but he claimed it did, and wrote it down. He relates to everything.

"He asked about the trees along the river. Nearly *every one* of them. I'd answer willow...hackberry...ash...catclaw...and now boxelders here at Saddle Canyon. He wanted the scientific names of everything.

"He saw cactuses up on the cliffs. That was easy. Then the sacred datura—with big, tubular white flowers—on a sand dune. He asked if the Indians used it. I said yes, to induce hallucinations. *That* set him off. I thought I'd *never* get out of that one. He kept asking: Pourquoi? Pourquoi? Pourquoi? Why? Why? Why?

"He asked about fish in the river. There, we got lost. The poor little Thai had no translations for chub and squawfish. When we passed Vasey's Paradise, he got started on springs in arid canyons. Do these springs have vegetation like we saw at Vasey's? Sure, I said. Maidenhair—most delicate of ferns. Monkeyflowers, yellow and crimson. Golden columbine, watercress, cardinal flower, orchids, grapevines... Before we got out of that one, the little Thai nearly collapsed, too."

I interrupted. "Neff, you are the hero of this expedition. That's *exactly* the kind of thing Chala wants. Believe me, he'll take it all back and use it to support nature reserve projects everywhere. I can understand your exhaustion..."

Neff slumped. "Thank you, Barry. In between all the plants and animals—we saw herons, mallards, a hooded oriole—he probed into how we *protected* wild animals. How our statutes got on the books. How we set aside such a vast landscape where the animals could roam in peace. Where every animal had *legal rights.* He focused on our policy of

humans being the intruders. He liked that. Asked me to explain it a dozen times."

"How did you?"

"I merely said that national parks are places where plants and animals live without human encroachment of any kind."

Neff paused, as though to prepare for a storm. "Then he asked, 'You allow fishing?' I said yes. He tore into me with a vengeance. Said I spoke with two tongues. How could I profess to protect wild animals and then allow fish to be killed? Aren't they wild animals? How could I do it? How? How? I couldn't answer. He asked if I liked to hunt. I said yes. He said, 'How could you? Don't you have any *feeling* for animals? No morals? No ethics? You Americans have two faces...' And on it went..."

"Just the same," I said, "he thinks our policies, even if faulty, are very good, indeed."

Neff: "Oh, he's good natured enough. But some of his questions are murder."

I barked: "Don't say that!"

"Oops!"

After we had served ourselves steak, beans and salad, I said: "I'd be interested in the response of this group to his proposal...giving animals legal rights."

Angel said at once: "I've been thinking about it. Sounds like a fundamental right to me...a planetary right. Why not?"

Ted Quail usually didn't say much, but he tore into Angel on that remark. "The hell! You think animals are more important than man?"

Angel looked at me. "That's not what Chala's proposing, is it?"

"No," I responded, "but that's how it's being misconstrued. Any time you want to give animals some increased rights, there's someone around to fight it. Parks and refuges go through that at inception. My question to you all is, just how you feel about it personally."

Ted Quail again: "Stinks. Stinks to high heaven. Happens over and over. Every goddam piss-ant wants to take my gun away from me."

Angel: "What kind of gun do you have?"

"Thirty Ought Six Springfield. And three others."

"Three other rifles?"

"Yes."

"Why?"

"I like guns."

"You like to hunt?"

"Yeah. Sure."

"Kill?"

"Yeah."

"Joe?"

"Three seventy five H and H Magnum."

"Woody?

"Mauser sporter."

"Julie?"

"No gun. I don't hunt."

"Neff?"

"I hunt. Winchester two seventy."

"Eddie?

"Ruger seven millimeter Magnum."

Pete Slattery, the equipment handler, and probably, at eighteen, the youngest person on the trip, made his answer in turn. "I ain't got enough money to buy a gun, or I'd have a Marlin thirty thirty."

Angel frowned. "There. You see? The worship of the gun. How can Chala fight that? It's universal."

"Well, don't misunderstand, Angel," said Neff, "I'm for Chala. I like to hunt, but I'd give it up if we could get universal rights on the books. India seems to do it all right."

Ted: "Yeah. Cow shit all over the streets. Monkeys in your hair."

Eddie Roff: "Bearing arms is a fundamental right."

Julie Baxter hopped on that one: "Is killing a fundamental right?"

Ted: "What you talkin' about? What's a gun for?"

Julie looked at me. "I see Chala's point now. He just wants the killing of wild animals stopped. His proposal has nothing whatever to do with guns."

Ted: "The hell! That's what it comes down to."

Angel: "Baloney. He doesn't care *how* you kill. There's a helluva lot of murder without guns. They snare elephants, trap foxes, hook fishes—."

Ted erupted. "You *see?* Next thing, they'll take our goddam fishin' rods from us!"

Joe: "A lot of countries do already. That's killing. That's contrary to law in a lot of parks and refuges. I've never understood how Americans can allow fishing in their national parks."

Ted rose in a huff, blurting: "I give up!" and walked off.

Suddenly Eddie Roff sat upright. "Oh my God, look there!"

They turned to look at him, then followed his gaze up river.

Chala strode along the shore, blue silk robe shining brightly in the dimming light.

Joe Muck sputtered: "*Ma foi!*" He jumped up and loped down the beach to Chala.

"Mon Eminence! Mon Eminence! Qu'est ce que nous avons ici? Nous avons un petit peur de danger!"

The hell, Joe said to himself, *we have more than a little danger.*

Chala replied imperiously: "Joseph, mon petit pauvre ami. Je voudrais simplement faire une promenade royale."

"Well," Joe told him, "royal promenade or not, you have to get back to your camp. You're a sitting duck here."

Chala bowed, said "Je compris, Joseph. I understand," and left, adding a bid for good night as he disappeared in the gloom.

I came up. "What the hell?"

"He just wanted a royal promenade."

I slapped my forehead. "If we get him out of this canyon alive—."

"If?" Joe asked. "Guess you're right. That's a bigger *if* than I thought."

After dinner, Joe and Julie walked along the beach to check with the guards.

"Ted Quail's pretty strong-willed," she commented.

"Most westerners are," Joe responded.

"How do *you* feel?" she asked. "You're on Chala's side, yet you hunt. You carry a gun. You're even a marksman."

He answered without hesitation. "I'm with Neff. I like it. It's the way I am. If I had to choose, though, I'd go for the animals."

"You'd give up guns?"

"I don't have to do that. The question is, would I stop killing?"

"Would you?"

"I could."

She pondered that answer as they walked in silence. They came to Cynthia Kasbolt.

Julie asked: "Everything quiet?"

"Light on the river." Cynthia pointed. "Canoe, I think."

"Keep it in sight," cautioned Joe. "Don't let it near."

"Roger," said Cynthia, and melted into the darkness again.

Near the Chala compound they met B. J. Pritchett.

"All okay?" Joe asked.

"They're bedding down."

Julie said: "You missed our discussion at dinner. Angel got the rangers and raft crew going on Chala's proposal. Ted Quail got pretty hot under the collar."

"That doesn't surprise me," B. J. commented. "Didn't want his gun taken away, right?"

"You got it," Joe answered. "What about you? Do you hunt?"

"I do."

Julie: "What kind of gun do you have?"

"Custom Remington. Why?"

"Oh, they were comparing. The implication was that if you have a gun, then you must be against Chala's proposal."

B. J. spoke candidly. "I have a different focus. Growing up black in Mississippi, all I could see was poverty ahead. One day I went on a school trip to Sabine National Wildlife Refuge in Louisiana. I saw the rangers taking care of the alligators. Protecting herons and egrets. I wanted to be a ranger."

"You did what you wanted," Julie said. "Good for you!"

"To me, it's a matter of freedom. Chala can do as he pleases. But I want to do as I please, too. We blacks had to win our freedom from slavery. We had to win our freedom from discrimination. Now I don't like someone taking my rifle away."

Julie: "It's not a matter of——."

"I know. It's not about guns. But what's a gun worth if you're not allowed to shoot anything with it? Like it or not, that's the kind of opposition psychology he has to deal with."

Joe asked: "What did you think—riding with him in the boat all day?"

"Nothing really. I respect him for trying. He's brave. He's having a good trip. That's what we're supposed to guarantee. But his ideas bother me—making animals equal to man."

Julie: "He hasn't said that—"

"He doesn't have to."

B. J. left and disappeared in the shadows.

The moon came up over the distant rim at nine o'clock, long before the last dregs of daylight had vanished. The yellow of sunset had poured like melted gold down the higher cliffs, changed to orange, then red, then purple, and faded in the veil of dusk.

"I never cease to be overwhelmed by the beauty of this place," Julie said softly. "I've never been so relaxed as here."

Joe asked: "Even when you're picking up bodies at the bottoms of cliffs?"

"Oh, people mean so little sometimes. These rocks have been here for hundreds of millions of years. What are we? Human beings have been here maybe a million years? Big deal."

Joe had never heard that kind of perspective before, except in astronomy books. He said nothing, hoping she would go on.

"When you reduce human beings to that insignificance," she said, "you feel a kind of peace you never knew before. The rocks don't change rapidly. Deer don't murder. Those bighorns back there—they don't bother *anyone*. Isn't it nice to be around such creatures?"

Joe's mind opened to her world. "You're never lonely, are you?"

Julie shook her head, a bit surprised at the question. "How could I be?"

"You don't get upset easily?"

"By human beings? By deer?"

"Not by anything?" he asked.

"Not by anything," she answered. "Why should I?"

Joe stretched his mind. "Then by that reasoning, you're not even afraid of death itself."

She stopped and looked at him squarely in the eyes. "When you have lived," she said, "and I mean *lived*—like walking these trails and riding this river in the most beautiful scenery on earth—then death is nothing. And you don't even think of it..." She paused a few moments. "Does that seem strange to you?"

"Strange?" he asked. "Nothing could be more familiar. I've thought the same things while riding my horse in the Sunlight Basin up in Wyoming."

"Then you're never lonely, either?"

"No. Never."

"What's your horse's name?"

"Dusty."

"That's a nice name. I like it."

Chala slept superbly.

"That's what bothers me," Dalton Stubbs said as they stood with bowls of cereal around the breakfast table. "We all swelter and sweat until three a.m., and he sleeps like a log."

Ted Quail said: "Why not? He grew up in the jungle. Had hot nights all his life."

"Well, not necessarily," I said. "Tropical nights can be pretty cool."

"Bullshit. I don't believe it."

I said, in a calm voice, "They don't usually have as many rocks as this to absorb the heat by day and let it back out at night."

Neff Neilson changed the subject. Picking up a plate of bacon, beans, hotcakes and hash browns, he said: "We've got another hot day ahead. Looks like it'll be clear and hot all day. Could get up to a hundred and ten."

"I'm going back to Bryce," said Cynthia Kasbolt.

Neff continued: "We have now come forty-seven miles. In another fifteen we will reach the junction of the Little Colorado River, which drains a lot of northeastern Arizona, including the Painted Desert and the Petrified Forest. In spring runoff it gets very big and very muddy, but that's about over now. It will be a light blue and we will stop for several hours so that you can have some long swims and lunch and relaxation."

"Does that mean sleep?" asked Eddie Roff.

Neff smiled. "Sure does! After that we'll make an afternoon run to Unkar Creek for camp. This is also your last day of light rapids..."

"Light?" asked Dalton Stubbs.

"It gets hairy tomorrow," Neff answered, "as we enter the Inner Gorge."

We fell to eating. Sam came up to me. "Ted's still a little testy."

I shrugged: "Oh, he's all right, Sam. He's giving us a good trip, and I told him I appreciate that. He's just a little nervous about anything that he perceives threatens to take his gun away from him."

"Well, a lot of the passengers are tired this morning. I can tell it on their faces. They were either on patrol, or they didn't sleep well."

"Or both," I added.

"They won't be very alert today. That cause for concern?"

"Sam, everything's cause for concern. But they all got a little sleep, at least. I'll have to be more alert."

"How did *you* sleep?"

"I haven't the slightest idea."

"Out like a log. Barry, you have no right to sleep like that. How do you do it?"

"Sam, I learned long ago how to sleep with one eye closed and stay alert with the other."

Sam snorted. "I don't believe a word of that. Not a word."

After breakfast, we brought tents and baggage to the rafts, loaded by passing luggage along a supply line, and got aboard. The temperature seemed almost cold by comparison with last night. No sun reached us yet. The beach still lay in deep shadow, illuminated only by the bright light of cliffs seen through dark portals. The surface of the river reflected the cliffs as in a black mirror.

"Let's go, everybody!" Joe shouted, pulling on a light jacket and then his life jacket. "We're about to get wet again. The sooner to sunlight, the better!"

"Not for a while," said Rudy Vogel. "You're gonna git *cold!*"

Sure enough, though the rapids seemed small, enough spray flew through the air—helped by a morning breeze—to set us shivering. The most red-eyed passengers, the ones on midnight patrol, curled up against the cargo.

I worried. On a river so busy, a murderer could hide with ease and strike at will. Now, to complicate matters, the crew had become exhausted. Concentrating on scenery, watching for danger, running the rapids, and now lack of sleep, had worn them down. In such a state of lassitude, could they stay awake, watch for signs of danger?

I looked up, trying to comprehend the massive scale of cliffs, the brilliance of sunlight, the depth of shadows. The far rim to the east now rose almost four thousand feet above the river. In the pure morning air, the lines of cliffs and rims stood out sharp and clear.

The three rafts floated peacefully on the glassy surface. Looking behind us, I saw two yellow oar-powered rafts come into view.

My hackles rose. I turned to get a better view.

Ted Quail's outspoken opposition to the Chala proposal bothered me. Quail had no desire to understand the proposal, or even discuss its purposes or limitations. He perceived only a threat from it. A threat to him. A threat to the entire fraternity of hunters. Something that might not actually occur for centuries. But, in Ted's mind, the danger lay here and now.

For me, the problem rested not with Quail alone, but with others the boatman might inflame. The protective force of rangers could be trusted, of course, but what about casual conversation along the river? Between rafts? At stopping points?

I could not rule out the passing of misinformation, the swell of indignation, the flash point of action... Or, worse yet, the vulnerability of Chala to hired killers mingling among the crowds. Suddenly I wished I had eyes in the back of my head.

We arrived at the junction at midmorning. The two rivers came together in a spectacular setting. The aquamarine color of the Little Colorado River provided a sharp contrast with the deep green Colorado into which it flowed.

Across the Colorado from the junction rose the massive promontory of Chuar Butte. Before the passengers could disembark, Neff said: "We're now at the beginning of the Grand Canyon proper. Chuar Butte up there has nearly all the rock formations to be found in the main canyon. On top is the Kaibab formation, then the Toroweap, then the yellowish Coconino sandstone forming sheer cliffs, then the steps and ledges of the red Supai group, the sheer face of the Redwall, the Muav limestone, the green of the Bright Angel shale and, at bottom, the Tapeats sandstone. The entire Paleozoic sequence. Where else can you see that? This is a geologist's paradise!"

Leaving the rafts, we found the junction a lively place. Wide platforms and sandy stretches up the Little Colorado offered places to reorganize gear, repair rafts, boats, canoes and kayaks, swim, and relax in the sun. Upstream, the Little Colorado flowed against limestone ledges and Tamarix groves, disappearing in deep and tortuous canyons to the east.

I talked with visitors, the staff, Chala, Woody. After the last encounter I worked my way among rafts, tarps, and oars. Passengers sprawled on the sand. I walked straight up to Buck Stevens, who sat on a ledge talking with Sam Petrie.

"You scoundrel!" My voice contained both surprise and indignation. "Woody just told me you have a Ph.D in outdoor recreation management"

Buck's face remained a mask. "Woody talks a lot."

"Why didn't you tell us?"

"It wasn't important."

"The hell it isn't!" I turned to Sam, nodding toward Buck. "Sam, here's a guy who's in charge of river use, could have a top-paying job just about anywhere, have everything he wants..."

Sam smiled wryly. "Maybe he *has* everything he wants."

I frowned. "Of coure he has. But why be selfish? With all the world's problems of endangered species, poaching and illegal exports, we need a mind like his *there*, not *here*. Not here where everything's already protected..."

Sam waved a hand toward me. "I agree, God knows. But we need top people here. Cool off. It's a free country. He can work wherever he wants."

Buck said to me, grinning. "We could use you here. And Joe."

Sam exploded and turned squarely toward him. "Now see here, Buck. You keep your mitts off Barry and Joe!"

Buck grinned. "You were just saying..."

Sam: "Never mind that!"

Buck: "Well, you gotta admit this is a pretty nice place to work."

"But why?" I asked. "Give me one good reason why you should stay here."

Buck said nothing. He pointed toward the river.

I became indignant. "That's selfish!"

Buck: "Sure. Why not?"

"You could be in any of a hundred countries, helping them sort out park management and wildlife protection. You could be instrumental in saving the tiger, the panda, the elephant. Do research. Hunt for rare species. Buck, we're short of good men."

"So are we."

B. J. Pritchett made his way to them. "Not much we can do with Chala," he said. "The guy violates every rule we lay down. He won't stay in the area we secured. He's always trotting off to meet someone else..."

I took B.J. by the arm. "He's a real gadfly, B.J. You're doing the best you can. I know what you're up against. His bodyguards are with him."

"Just the same—."

"I would appreciate it, B.J., if you would follow along to see that they *stay* with him."

"Yes, sir."

"We can only hope for the best."

"I have the rangers deployed. Looking for suspicious characters."

"Finding any?"

B.J. answered: "All over the place,"and walked away.

Sam Petrie laughed aloud. "Can't keep these guys down! Are there that many bad people on the river?"

Buck closed his eyes in mock despair, then raised an eyebrow as he looked at Sam. "Microcosm. We get all kinds. But mostly they're a pretty good lot."

"You've made my point," I said. "We need people with your education to help deal with the *really* bad lots. Your experience..."

"Don't put that much in it," Buck said.

"But your degree..."

"Bullshit. I can show you guys with degrees who aren't—."

"I know all that. I have one myself. I know better."

"Now you surprise *me!*"

"That's a twist."

"Well, Barry, there's some Ph.Ds I sure as hell wouldn't *want* to send to some other country."

"Granted. But you miss my point. Why do you want to stay here?"

"Because I *like* it here. I like the river. The people."

"You could have anything you want."

"This is where we came in."

Sam Petrie laughed. I said: "All right. I'll change the subject. Let me ask you. About this trip—what do you think? Can we get Chala through?"

Buck answered: "How many people after him?"

"Don't know."

"Hit squads?"

"Yes. But we think they don't know where he is."

"Far behind?"

"Probably."

"What kinds of hit squads?"

"International fur trade, probably. Illegal export—tiger bone, that sort of thing."

"Sophisticated?"

"Very."

"Okay. We have some dangerous spots ahead where protection is practically impossible."

"Such as?"

"Bridges across the river. Heavily traveled trails beside the river. Good vantage points. Just the right range for rifles.

"And we stop at Phantom Ranch. Busy place."

Buck lifted his cap and ran his fingers through his hair. "Want my advice?"

"Of course."

"Turn back here."

At this, Sam Petrie guffawed again. "Back? This guy's got you, Barry. There ain't no way back. The Colorado's a river of no return."

"I know that," I said. "And so does Buck."

Julie and Joe asked Cass and Tillie Wyberger, young kayakers, if they had seen anything suspicious on the river.

"Yeah," said Cass, peeling off his dark blue wet suit. "There's three guys in a pink oar raft. Noisy. They have guns. We saw them shooting."

Julie bristled. "On the river?"

"Yes, ma'am."

"That is illegal enough to give them real problems. Are they here now?"

"They went up the Little Colorado half an hour ago."

"Can you describe them?"

"One beard. One stubble. One gray and black hair."

"Thanks. You going to be around here for a while?"

"Drying stuff out."

"Well, I would appreciate it if you'd let me know the minute they get back."

"Glad to."

Julie and Joe walked on. "That could be ominous," he said.

"Don't count on it," she replied. "We get types like that on the rims. Shoot up signs. Break into cars. Steal credit cards..."

"In a national park?"

"Sure. Tourists are careless. They think we have our arms around them."

"You don't often get international hit squads?"

"Tell me about them."

"Everybody keeps one eye on the UN. The minute it proposes something that could even remotely injure some industry, the goons come out. Offer themselves for hire."

"Professional killers?"

"Sometimes they're professional. They call themselves 'lobbyists'."

"How will you know when you see them?"

"We won't. All we know is what the international security agencies tell us. Some kind of a squad is after Chala. We don't think they know he's in the Grand Canyon."

Julie thought a moment. "Unless there's an informant inside Chala's UNEP office."

They watched families splashing in the light blue waters of the Little Colorado. Joe said: "Let's go swim."

"I'm in uniform," she said.

"That's okay," he responded. "It'll dry out."

Evie Lund, the nurse, interrupted them. "I've been watching Chala."

They saw Chala conversing vigorously with a cluster of river runners at the shore of the Colorado. "He's wearing that cowboy hat now, but he doesn't like to wear hats. He keeps taking it off in the raft."

"For short periods?" Joe asked.

"Too many short periods. The hat falls off when he looks up. And anyway, he thinks the cool air above the river protects him from the sun."

"So?"

"If someone doesn't get to him, he's going to have a heat stroke."

Joe let out a long whistle. "That would be ironic."

Evie frowned. "Ironic?"

"He's got all these guys after his scalp...and the sun gets it instead. I'll talk to him. Anything else?"

"Someone should watch him on hikes. He has a nerve-wracking habit of putting his hand on ledges without looking."

"Looking for what?"

"Rattlesnakes. That's where they sleep. In the shade."

"C'mon. I'm told the Grand Canyon rattlesnake isn't very aggressive."

"You want Chala to find out what it does when someone reaches out and puts a hand on it?"

"All right, Evie. I appreciate your concern. I'll speak to him. What about first aid?"

"Kit in each raft. Why?"

"We'd better carry first aid when he goes away from the raft."

Julie spoke up. "That's a good idea. But not to worry too much. We seldom see any rattlers down here."

Evie left, only to be replaced by a couple of river runners approaching Julie. "Ranger, who *is* that?" one asked, pointing to Chala.

"African prince," she replied."

"Oo-oo!" the other said. "Exciting. Let's go see him!"

Joe rolled his eyes into the air. "This has gotten out of hand. Can't we get him back into the security area?"

"He won't go," Julie answered.

"You can make him."

"You want us to?"

Joe paused. "No. I have another idea..."

They walked over to the crowd surrounding Chala and the bodyguards.

Joe raised his voice. "Sorry, folks. I've got to take our distinguished guest from Africa away for a press interview. He's so busy, you know. Thank you for your interest. Goodbye."

Chala looked puzzled.

Joe explained: "Mon Eminence, il nous faut avoir un petit entrevue avec la presse, s'il vous plait."

Chala brightened. "Très bien, Joseph. Très bien! Allons!"

Joe took Chala's arm, whispering as he passed Julie: "That was easy. He's a publicity hound!"

Kathi LeClair, raised in France by American parents, remembered French sufficiently to conduct an interview. She accompanied Chala to a small cove in the rock wall, and talked with him while the bodyguards and Julie Baxter sealed off entry. Dietrich Deitemeyer and Tip Phrakonekham seized the opportunity to escape from Chala's side and go for a swim.

Passing me, Joe whispered: "Have the Wybergers—that couple over there—notify you and Buck when the Goons come back."

"What are you talking about?" I asked.

Joe disappeared around the corner. I asked Buck: "What the hell was that all about?"

Buck grinned. "Guess we'd better ask the Wybergers."

Kathi LeClair had so many questions already sketched in her notebook that she didn't know where to begin. Chala obliged by a long peroration on his village, his family, the animals he loved, his long road to UNEP. No one could stop him. Kathi wrote furiously, lapsing into shorthand for direct quotes.

When Chala paused for breath, she asked at once whether he knew how much flak he'd been getting.

"Le flak! Le flak! Certainement, ma petite. Il y en a beaucoup. Je le sais."

But flak didn't stop him. He went on, and gave her a frills-free description of his proposal.

Did he see any hope of success?

Certainement!

In his lifetime?

Posiblement.

That's asking a great deal, she told him. That's very fast...to turn around the whole world's thinking. Why was he doing such a difficult thing?

Because too many people are killing too many animals. He implored Joe to explain to her the plight of the tiger.

Kathi held up her hand. "I know," she said. Then, lapsing into French again, she asked whether any one else shared his views.

"Tout le monde!" he replied.

But surely he couldn't mean *everybody*, she said. Whereupon he asked whether she knew anyone who wanted to see another species become extinct.

Some people don't care, she answered. They care only for the fur trade that gives them jobs now.

So! he shot back. Where will the fur trade be without fur?

They don't care! she snapped. All they want is to preserve their own jobs, their own money, their own—.

The exchange grew livelier than Joe expected. Their voices echoed from the walls of the little cove as from an amphitheater. River runners, astonished at hearing a vigorous conversation in French here at the bottom of the Grand Canyon, collected even more than before, so pressing against Julie for a closer view that she had to signal Cynthia Kasbolt, the nearest ranger, for reinforcements.

"What are they talking about?" came queries from the crowd.

Julie raised her voice. "Folks, if you don't mind, he's a prince from West Africa and he's being interviewed for the *Arizona Daily Sun*. You can read all about it when you leave the canyon. It'll probably go national. Right now, I'd appreciate it if you could back up, and let's just leave them alone. May we, please?"

The crowd dispersed. Julie turned and caught Kathi's eye, then moved her hands in a damping motion to suggest keeping their voices lower.

Kathi nodded, then turned back to Chala, telling him that his quest seemed like an impossible dream.

"Imposible?" he shot back, raising his voice again. "Imposible?"

From here on, the conversation seemed to Joe to lapse into pure theater.

KATHI. How can you equate animals with man?

CHALA. Easy, my little one. Easy. Ah, but it was one of your own great writers...one of your most *revered* American writers...who said it far better than I could. Do you not know that?

KATHI. I'm confused. Said what? Who? When?

CHALA. You must take this down carefully, my little one.

KATHI. I will. I promise.

CHALA. Well, he said that the proper place of man is *below* the beast .

KATHI. An American writer said that? I don't believe it.

CHALA. Yes, he did...*below* the beast since man is always foul-minded and guilty, while the animals are clean-minded and innocent. *(Thumps breast.)* Hah! Did you know that? Your own favorite *Americain!* Man should be below the beast. *(Laughs heartily.)*

KATHI. *(Scoffing)* No, no. no. But I think that could be very true! Who? Who said that?

CHALA. Ah, ma petite, it was none other than your beloved Mark Twain.

KATHI. *(A trifle disappointed.)* Aw, but that's satire...

CHALA. *(Leaning closer.)* Do you remember all the satires about women?

KATHI. Yes.

CHALA. And now women have equal rights?

KATHI. Yes.

CHALA. Do you remember all the satires about blacks?

KATHI. Yes.

CHALA. And now blacks have equal rights?

KATHI. Yes.

CHALA. *(Lifting head quickly in princely fashion.)* Then the animals are next!

Joe exploded with laughter, flashing to Chala a thumbs up sign.

Kathi wrote furiously, not wanting a word of that exchange to escape. Then she abruptly changed the subject. What did he think of the Grand Canyon?

"Le plus magnifique, le plus grande, le plus étonnant, le plus ..."

She stopped these superlatives to ask whether such places, such wildlife refuges and parks, might some day encompass all endangered animals in the world. He grasped her hand and kissed it, saying that that would be a wonderful dream...a dream...a dream. You must write about it, he told her. Come to us at UNEP, tell the world—the whole world...

She did not know exactly how to stop this interview, and she did not really want to. Chala could be a reporter's dream.

Joe interrupted, seeing how repetitious the exchange had become.

"Mon Eminence, allons au plage?"

Chala's eyes brightened at the prospect of a swim. Joe and Julie led him away.

As they moved toward the upper, less crowded, end of the swimming area, Tillie Wyberger approached them, pointing upstream. "The Goons are coming back."

Julie motioned to Cynthia to take her place in the Chala transfer and detached herself to meet the "Goons," as the Wybergers called them. Joe followed.

The Goons met the Wybergers' descriptions: disheveled, bearded, slouched.

"Good morning," Julie called out as they splashed ashore. "Did you go up the canyon very far?"

Woody Watkins came up to listen in on the conversation.

"No," one of the men replied. "Too much work. Hee! Hee! Hee!"

"Many people up there?"

"No. Jest a few here and there."

Buck and I strode up to listen.

"Well," Julie went on. "You gentlemen having a good trip?"

"Yeah, yeah! Hee! Hee! Who you callin' gen'lmen, Miss?"

"You from around here?"

They looked at each other. "Around here?" one said, glancing at the canyon walls and exploding with a giggle. "Lordy, no!"

They all broke into laughter. Julie joined in the mirth, and when it subsided she asked: "Have to wait long for a trip permit?"

"Permit? Oh, yeah ... No, didn't wait long ..."

At that point they saw the cluster of rangers around Chala. "That the African prince they's all talkin' 'bout?"

"Yes," Woody answered.

"Which one's him?"

"Wearing the cowboy hat," Woody answered.

They broke into laughter again. "Can ya beat that? A African prince in a cowboy hat! Guess I seen everything, now." More raucous laughter.

Julie went on. "Well, about those permits. May I see them?"

The laughter died.

Joe watched Chala doff his hat and wade carefully out into the water. The bodyguards followed. Dietrich and Tip, the little Thai, joined them. The rangers remained on shore, pushing back the crowd and watching for weapons.

"Permits?"

Julie: "Yes, sir."

"Smoke? You got the permits?"

"No. I ain't got no permits?"

"Duke?"

"Whatcha lookin' at me fer? You know I ain't got no permits, Winnie."

Winnie turned back to Julie. "Well, ma'am. Nobody tol' us we'd have to have permits. We just drove up to Lee's Ferry and tuck our raft and putt her in the water."

Julie asked: "You read the signs?"

Another explosion of laughter. "Yeah! Hee, hee, hee! Smoke, he went and looked, but Smoke don't know how to read! Heh! Heh! Heh! Ain't that funny?"

"Not to me, it isn't," Woody broke in. "We have rules and regulations in this park. Ignorance of them is not a defense. If you have no permit, I will have to confiscate your boat at Phantom Ranch and you will be required to walk out from there. Miss Baxter will issue you a citation, which will be taken up in district court at a time of which you will be notified. I instruct you now to get in your raft and get to Phantom Ranch this afternoon. A ranger will be waiting there to take your raft into custody."

"But ... but we'uns ..."

"Gentlemen, I suggest you take off now. There are eight rangers here to assist if you need—."

"No. No. We're goin'. C'mon, Smoke. Duke, git your ass down to the boat and let's git outta here."

When they left, Julie strode to the Wybergers to thank them and to get a deposition from them regarding the behavior of the Goons as seen on the river.

"What will you do to them?" Tillie asked.

Buck answered, leaning over confidentially. "We takes 'em up to the rim, and goes to the edge, and jus' drops 'em off."

Tillie recoiled. "Oh, no! You couldn't!"

Buck stepped closer. "May I see your permit, please?"

Tillie leaped away, vaulted over two kayaks, and departed, shouting: "It's in the kayak. In the kayak! I'll be right back!"

Julie insisted that Buck apologize to Tillie Wyberger for such an outrageous story—which he did—to the relief of Cass and Tillie. The Babb Brothers—Winnie, Smoke, and Duke—left in their pink raft.

Chala completed his swim and went ashore in an admiring crowd. Aides brought him sandwiches. He sat to eat, surrounded by onlookers. With Tip, the little Thai, as interpreter, he told them stories of his childhood—"mon enfance dans la forêt"—and held them spellbound with his language and the drama of his tales, replete with lions, baboons, cheetahs and chimpanzees...the last experience one would anticipate at the junction of the Colorado and Little Colorado Rivers.

The rangers patrolled, watching every spectator, noting every backpack, spotting every suspicious move, until Ted Quail passed the word to load up.

"Tout va bien?" I asked Chala quietly, knowing full well that the prince had become mesmerized by the canyon and the people.

"Barry," Chala confided, softly and solemnly, "c'est la suprême experience de ma vie."

I said to myself: *Well, it would be the supreme experience of my life, too, if you weren't about to be murdered.*

As we moved out into the Colorado once more, and the current carried us beneath the imposing ramparts of Chuar Butte, I squinted in the bright light and began to assess our situation. So far, so good. And yet, a number of things bothered me. The Goons, for example. They seemed interested in Chala, what he looked like, what he wore. Too interested.

Then the matter of the violent rapids ahead. A raft could capsize. The antagonisms against Chala—made visible by sullen looks on certain faces, especially that of Ted Quail. Antagonisms sometimes have a way of growing, spreading...

Then, too, something Buck had said bothered me. Bridges across the river. Foot bridges. Mule bridges. I remembered them from my other trips into the canyon.

And the trails alongside the river. From them, an assassin would have splendid views down into open boats. Superb access to any of the passengers... And what could be done about it? Erect a bulletproof tent over the second raft? Encase Chala in protective vests?

No, there came a time when all efforts could fail, when nothing would shield our happy-go-lucky peripatetic passenger from grief. Well, Chala knew the risks...

And the cowboy hat. Joe had been right to give it to Chala. Everyone needed defense against the brutality of the desert sun. Yet what a symbol it had become! No matter the incongruity of an African prince in a cowboy hat. It marked a distinguished visitor. It could be seen from afar. And *it could lead a murderer directly to the target.*

If a killer waited downstream, I asked myself, how would he know that Chala wore a cowboy hat? Obvious, mon ami: word travels along this river faster than a speed boat.

A few inquiries—and any killer could have the man in his gun sight...his scope...

"I can tell what you're thinking," said Buck.

"Bet you can't," I responded.

"You're trying to figure how to get Chala under Kaibab Suspension Bridge without getting him shot."

"Buck, you're uncanny. Now give me a brilliant answer."

"Ain't none, as they say in the vernacular out here."

"What about after dark?"

"Run the Colorado River at night?"

"I take it back."

Buck pondered. "I've been thinking about the same thing, Barry."

"No answer?"

"None."

"Well then, station a couple of rangers at the bridge."

"We've exhausted the supply of available rangers for a radius of four hundred miles."

"Well, then, we'll have raft number one go ahead after breakfast tomorrow and when they get to Bright Angel Creek, they'll land and Joe and the rangers will come back upstream by trail to the bridge. That way they can cover Chala's passage underneath."

Buck thought about that for a moment. "Barry, you'd make a good ranger in this park."

I laughed. "That's what Woody said about Joe."

Sam Petrie, sitting beside them, admonished Buck: "You keep your mitts off Barry and Joe!"

"Well," said Buck, "there's a flaw in your plan. The other two rafts would be undermanned on the run from Unkar Creek to Phantom Ranch."

"I've already thought of that," I said, "so I've ruled the idea out. Anything else?"

Buck said: "Keep in mind that there are other problems along this river. We have to run Hance, Sockdologer, and

Grapevine Rapids tomorrow. Not the biggest, but they're there."

"Meaning?"

"We could capsize."

"Is that likely? With these big rafts?"

"No. But it happens."

"And if it does?"

"Everybody gets dumped out and lurches to the next pool."

"Dangerous?"

"Damn right. Everything's dangerous about this river. But why should that stop us?"

Sam said: "Can I get off at the next stop?"

It didn't take long to run the nine miles from the junction of the Little Colorado River to camp at Unkar Creek. The river widened, became shallow, and made a long turn to the west. The canyon opened up. From here we could see the South Rim at Desert View, more than five thousand feet above. On a broad shelf at the western edge of the river, we spread out and located our camp sites.

The afternoon sun sent blistering heat down upon us, moderated by a gentle breeze, as though from a furnace. The brave went wading. The tired went to sleep. The others dried out their equipment and prepared for tomorrow. They remembered Ted Quail's warning as they disembarked: "Rough day on the river tomorrow, starting right over there. Unkar Rapid has a drop of twenty-five feet."

"That's nothing," scoffed Sam.

Ted's eyes narrowed to slits. "Four miles beyond that is Hance. Class Eight."

Sam looked up at Quail. "Class Eight? Out of ten?"

Ted managed a sickly grin. "Out of ten," he answered.

Here at the end of the second day, the mood of Chala's aides became more tense. The strain of danger, hour after hour, outweighed, for some of them at least, the joy of the extraordinary landscape. At home in New York or Nairobi, working in secured buildings, they could relax. Here, with every crevice capable of harboring someone who could shower them with bullets, they felt uneasy, tired, exhausted.

Dietrich Deitemeyer, handling Chala's affairs, demanded a conference. Joe and I obliged, getting together Woody, B.J., Buck and Julie as experts on the river, the inner canyon, and park activities.

"What happens from here on?" Dietrich asked it in a belligerent tone. "Once and for all, let's get the schedule straight. Is this chaos—the kind of thing we experienced at the junction of the Little Colorado—to continue? All those crowds? That was terribly dangerous. You told us Chala was going to have maximum protection. What kind of protection is that? He could have been assassinated in that crowd. What are you going to do about it?"

Julie seemed surprised. "Chala did all that himself."

"Well, you must stop him."

"We did. We tried to confine him, for his own good. We tried our best to keep all those people away from him."

"Well, you didn't do it."

"We also tried to keep *him* away from *them*. No way. And besides, he had a ball. I watched him. He ate up all that adulation. He likes attention. He glorifies in it. You must certainly know that."

Joe added: "He even asked me if he should get out his blue robes and have a 'Presence Royale.' I told him he was enough of a Royal Presence as he was. He's exuberant. How the hell are you going to protect a person like that? I mean *really* secure him?"

Dietrich frowned. "That is not my job. It is *your* job."

Joe scowled. His voice indicated controlled anger. "On this trip, protecting Chala is everybody's job."

"Nevertheless, you do not answer my question."

Buck took over. As the river ranger, he would be most knowledgeable. "The people going down this river," he said, with a tone of conviction, "are mostly honest, good-natured, respectful. Some of the finest in the world..."

"Mostly? Mostly?" Dietrich waved his arm through the air. "What about the rest? Those other few? We always worry about *them*."

Buck tactfully sidestepped. "Well, I think you are aware that there are dangers in this canyon. We have some rough rapids tomorrow morning. The kind of thrill people come for..."

"Dangerous? How dangerous?"

Buck began to tire of this tone. "We refer to this river's characteristics as challenges. Is this not what Chala wants?"

"Yes, yes, of course. Will we turn over? Set up? I mean upset?"

Buck nodded matter-of-factly. "We could."

Dietrich blurted: "We *could?* Why did you not—?"

"You can turn over on a highway, in an airplane, in a raft. Of course. It's possible. We understand that Chala can swim..."

"Yes, yes. We all can. But this river is so powerful. It could dash us to pieces."

I thought of saying that the danger of being dashed to pieces on Roosevelt Drive near the UN building in Manhattan would be infinitely greater, but I left the matter to Buck.

"To answer your question," Buck continued, "we lunch tomorrow at the mouth of Bright Angel Creek, a short distance from Phantom Ranch. We can go on a short hike. Chala likes to hike, doesn't he?"

"Yes, yes."

"Well, then, that's a side-canyon type of experience he said he wanted."

"Good, good."

"Then, after lunch at Bright Angel Creek, we pass through a series of rapids—Granite, Hermit, Crystal. These are the closest we'll get to Class Ten."

Dietrich blanched and turned to Woody. "There! You see? We are not informed of all these dangers!"

I answered instead. "Yes, Dietrich, we were. The Interior Department sent us all the brochures and maps. They warned us of the dangers along this river. I thought you saw all of that."

"All right! All right! Go on."

Buck continued. "We will come to what I think are the most beautiful portions of the trip ... Stephen Aisle, Conquistador Aisle. We'll climb up to Elves Chasm, stop at Deer Creek Falls, and finally climb up past four waterfalls to the Havasupai Indian Village. That will be more than seven miles. Can Chala take it?"

"Yes, yes! He wants to see those people. But is it safe?"

"Then by horseback eight miles to Hualapai Hilltop. Can he ride a horse that far?"

"Yes. Is it safe? All that?"

I answered. "As safe as we can make it, Dietrich. That's the best we can do. If something happens, it happens. You know the problems. They're Chala's problems. Our problems. We can't expect the Department of the Interior to work miracles."

B. J. Pritchett said softly: "We'll try."

Woody added: "But we can't guarantee."

Buck said: "I suggest you forget the things that *could* happen and take what comes. Chala says he's having a supreme experience. Is that true?"

Dietrich nodded reluctantly.

"Then let's keep it that way."

"And one other thing," Julie said. "Could you keep his royal hands off the ledges and away from shady spots? There could be rattlesnakes in there...taking refuge from the heat."

"We'll try."

"And scorpions," she added. "Please counsel him not to pick up *anything* that crawls."

Dietrich: "What if he wants to?"

Julie scowled. "*Don't* let him."

"But——. He's always handled animals."

"*Not here.*"

Dietrich looked at her fiercely, then turned on his heel and left.

"Oh, my God!"

Cynthia Kasbolt turned and ran toward Joe and me.

"What's the matter?" I asked.

She pointed toward the river. "Now he's swimming!"

Sure enough, Chala had peeled to his swimsuit and begun to step in the swift-flowing water.

Ted Quail saw him at the same time. "GET HIM OUT OF THERE! THAT'S NOT SWIMMIN' WATER! THERE'S RAPIDS BELOW!"

Joe yelled: "EMINENCE! NON!" and took off.

As he leaped over rabbitbrush he flung off his hat and shirt.

Chala had not heard. Now up to his hips, he began to stagger under the hidden and unexpected force of the current.

"Eminence! Eminence!" Joe shouted.

The African lost his footing and sank to his neck, the torrent hurling him against sharp-edged sandstone layers underwater.

Joe, in one flying leap, pancaked on the surface and churned the waters like a motorboat until he could grasp Chala's arm. The icy water sent sharp pangs through his body.

Chala went under. Joe pulled him up, turned him toward shore. Within seconds, Buck and I hit the water, splashed up and grasped the other arm. By now we flowed along at a brisk pace, nearing the lip of the rapids. The powerful torrent made landing hazardous.

Joe grabbed a rock, spun around, lost hold of Chala. A current surge hurled Buck back. That left me. I lunged with superhuman energy, slammed my foot against a rock and thrust Chala out of the water. A Herculean task—using the leverage of a rock to move a big man against a powerful current. The force of the water threatened to upset a precarious balance and rip us both away to the churning maelstrom just below.

I pushed and thrust with every ounce of strength I had. Within moments we rolled into shallow water, crashing against boulders and slabs of submerged sandstone.

Cynthia Kasbolt and Julie Baxter raced up and helped pull Chala and me from the water. Evie Lund arrived with a towel and led us to the first aid kit. As soon as we had dried off the water and some of the blood, she applied antiseptic salves and bandages to the assorted cuts and scratches.

Julie stormed over to Dietrich, her eyes flashing. "He could have drowned all four of them! If he doesn't obey our instructions, and the orders of the boatmen, we'll handcuff him and tie him to the raft! I don't care who he is!"

Dietrich said: "I'm sorry, madam. I'm terribly sorry. I apologize. I will speak to him."

"And," she added, her voice still seething with rage, "if he has bodyguards, order them to stay with him or we'll tie *them* to the raft, too. Do I make myself clear?"

"Yes, sir. I mean, yes ma'am." Dietrich reddened and left.

After Joe had dried off and changed clothing, he walked with Julie along the river's edge. The sun poured evening gold over the Desert Palisades, a rim of sheer walls to the east.

"You were kinda tough on him."

"Let it happen again," she snapped, "and I'll *show* you what tough is. Let's change the subject."

"Okay. What's the North Rim like?"

"Higher," she answered. "Cooler. Forest of spruce and fir. Kaibab squirrels. Pretty remote, some of it."

"I'd like to take a horseback trip through part of that some time."

"Why not just hike?"

"I like hiking. I like horses, too."

"I guess you would, being a rodeo star."

"Who said I was a rodeo star?"

"Aren't you?"

"Well, I haven't been in the chute for more than a year now."

"You going back to it?"

"Naw. My spine is still in one piece. I think I'll keep it that way."

"You miss it, though?"

"Sure. It's exciting. Gets your adrenalin up. Out of the gate. Ride like hell. Off you go. Into the dust. Bronc falls on you. Ruins your whole day."

"Must be great fun."

"You do any riding in Kentucky?"

"A little."

"You don't like horses?"

"I like not horses less but hiking more."

"You're pulling a Byron on me."

"Well, it's true."

"Okay. I'll get weaned. Some day. What else did you do?"

She thought for a moment. "Some spelunking..."

"Caving? Really?"

"Yeah, except they don't like women in mines and caves in ol' Kaintuck."

"Why not?"

"Well, because they're women."

"I thought that kind of stuff had gone out..."

"Not in ol' Kaintuck. Doesn't matter, though. I went down anyway. Some beautiful caves."

"I want to see them."

"You want to see everything."

He laughed. "I will, too!"

When they got back, they checked on Chala resting comfortably, full of remorse. Joe chatted with him briefly to assure him of no hard feelings.

At the dinner table, the rangers' conversation had turned, as it often does among rangers, to tourists and their foibles.

"When I was at Joshua Tree National Park," said Dalton Stubbs, "this woman comes up and asks about all those blue flowers she'd seen. And I tell her they're fringed gentians. So she goes back to her family and says: "The ranger says they're fringed genitals.""

The crowd erupted in riotous laughter.

Mozo Fernandez added: "We put up a sign at Old Faithful in Yellowstone saying that the next eruption of the geyser would be at such-and-such an hour. But some people don't even see the sign. One day a guy came rushing up and asks 'When's your next erection?'"

Eddie Roff said: "When I was at Carlsbad Caverns, people were always asking, 'Ranger, is this cave all underground?'"

Joe: "You're making that up."

"I'm not. Happens all the time. And if it wasn't that, they'd ask: 'Ranger, how many miles of this cave are undiscovered?'"

Cynthia: "Don't people *ever* stop to think before they ask?"

Angel Ingebretson, the historian, said, "Hah! I'll tell you! At Edison National Historic Site in New Jersey, there's a sign...a real favorite of Edison's...a quote by Sir Joshua Reynolds: *There is no expedient to which a man will not resort to avoid the real labor of thinking.*"

Neff said: "Wonderful! I like that. We get people here to the Canyon, drive up in a rush and ask us 'Ranger, we got an hour to see Grand Canyon. What should we do first?' And I tell them, 'Sit down and weep.'"

"You won't believe this," Eddie Roff added, "but one time when I was stationed in the King's Palace, one of the lower chambers in Carlsbad Caverns, a man comes in and says to his wife, 'Hey, we're in the King's Palace.' And his wife says, 'How do you know that, dear?' And he says, 'I saw it on the sign.' And she says, 'Oh, I never read signs. You can get into trouble that way.'"

Cynthia: "Is that true?"

"I'm not kidding," he replied. "I heard it myself."

Angel said, "I don't doubt anything any more. Back in the early mining days, some prospectors had a camp on Horseshoe Mesa, below Grandview Point. They had tents set up, and a cook to prepare evening meals when they got back late.

"One night in August, the miners sat on their haunches outside after dinner, watching a meteor display. They'd point and shout and jabber that Judgment Day was nigh, and worked themselves into a frenzy believing that heaven itself was about to fall.

"The cook came out and saw what was going on, turned back into the cook tent, scooped up a shovelful of red-hot clinkers from the stove, sneaked out behind the miners and listened for a minute. When the right time came, and a swarm of shooting stars zapped through the sky, he chucked the whole shovelful of clinkers as high as he could.

"They came whizzing down right in front of the miners. One of the men leaped up, grabbed one of the clinkers, tried to hold on to it, and shouted, 'A shootin' star fell! A shootin' star fell! Feel it! It's still hot!' He brought it over to the cook to show what he'd found.

"Well, one of the boys took that clinker to the park museum and it was labeled as a meteorite, until the cook, years later, went to the park naturalist and told the story."

Dinner ended and darkness came, but the stories went on in a seemingly endless flow, until finally B.J. said, "We better hit the sack. Tomorrow's going to be a rough day."

We left Unkar Creek camp at nine the next morning. The sun had already climbed high in the sky, its blistering rays softened by an overcast.

Almost at once, we fell off into Unkar rapid, skewing and thumping in a drop of twenty-five feet over a distance of nearly five hundred yards. Enough to wet us with spray and start us out shivering, despite the filtered sunlight.

Then some riffles, then Nevills rapid, and, in short order, we approached the lip of Hance rapid, Class Eight, a drop of thirty feet in three hundred yards.

"Hang on with both hands!" Ted Quail warned.

Joe, on the prow of the first raft, looked down with thrill and trepidation.

"Are we gonna git our asses wet on *this* one!" he shouted.

The roaring waters fell into troughs, then exploded into waves that curled backward and sent up fountains of foam and spray. Not far down the rapid, the waters washed against a huge chunk of sandstone that had come to rest in the midst of the most violent current.

Joe found himself hoping that Ted had memorized exactly how and where to plunge off into this maelstrom. If not, if they got pushed the wrong way by those currents, they could run broadside into that rock, get caught there and be pinned down by the roaring waters.

Once off the lip, Joe figured, the raft would be almost beyond control. If it tipped into a trough the wrong way, got pushed from starboard and thrown sideways, it could flip over and hurl them all out, where they would sink out of sight in the foaming mass.

He caught a quick glance of Ted's face. Calm but concentrating mightily at the breakaway point. Joe felt reassured. At a time like this, he thought, it's always nice to know that *someone* is in control. Even if they went out of control. But he only felt reassured for a moment. He took a quick camera shot and plunged the camera into its rubber bag.

The raft glided off and seemed momentarily to shoot straight out into empty air. Then the front fell with a *SMACK!* into the trough and struck the rolling ridge of water on the other side.

Up went a curtain of spray, followed by a mountain of water. Tons of it, or so it seemed. Water suddenly came down on all sides, buried the passengers briefly, and passed on to the rear.

The raft shot out of the water, the nose climbing into the sky. There it poised a moment, and then, caught by a tail current, skewed around, swerved sideways, and fell with a slap! into the next trough, burying the passengers in another cascade.

Joe shook his head to fling the water out of his eyes. His shriek of "Ai-yee-ee!" got curdled by the foam and came out "Ai-yulpp!"

For a moment, he saw them skidding directly toward the big boulder, but the downstream flow bore the raft past, missing the rock by less than three feet.

Before they could recover their composure, another bathtub of icy water drowned them momentarily. The raft yawed, whipped its tail, clawed for the sky again, went down with a resounding *THUMP!*, and shifted sideways.

The cargo surged against the ropes. The bindings creaked with the strain. The left side of the raft rose, tipping them at a scary angle of at least thirty-five degrees, pitching the passengers either sideways or bottoms up, sending their legs into the air, gliding through the waves at a furious pace.

"Ai-ee-yulpp!" Joe blurted.

They settled momentarily back to normal. The worst (or best) had ended, but the craft still shook in the waves farther on, tipped down again, shot up in the air, tilted, wavered...and went on.

"Whee!" Joe shouted as the waves subsided. "Good show, Ted!"

The Chala raft went over with the same wild gyrations, the passengers gripping ropes, their feet flying high, their bodies buried in a sudden Niagara of falling water.

Then our raft went over, Sam saying at the lip of the fall: "I think I'll get off here."

By the time the three rafts had reached the bottom and calmed down again, the passengers—soaked, shaken, and definitely wide awake—found themselves shouting at once. Including Chala, who called over to Joe, with something of a sputter: "Incroyable, Cowboy! Inoubliable! Étonnant!"

"Moi, aussi!" Joe called back. "Le même chose! Inoubliable!" He meant it. He thought of the experience as incredible, unforgettable, and astonishing...and all the other adjectives you could bring up. Even Dietrich, sitting beside Chala, sent a thumbs up signal.

Banging and bumping, the rafts careened on down the length of Hance, leaving the passengers completely soaked.

Less than a mile later we "battened the hatches" again for Sockdologer.

The rapids came in quick succession. By the time we got doused again in Sockdologer and twisted our way down the long descent of Grapevine, we had become both wet and chilled. Filtered sunlight through the overcast didn't help very much. The black walls of crushed and folded gneisses and schists in the Inner Gorge seemed only to add to the gloom.

After Grapevine, we all huddled in bundles aboard the rafts, shivering and waiting for the landing at Bright Angel Creek.

Joe got out his rifle.

He did not like the idea of taking this group under a suspension bridge close to the water. Neither did I. We had no choice. We would all be as vulnerable as ducks on a pond. And I could do very little about it. Were I to assassinate someone, the bridge would be an ideal location from which to shoot and run. Nobody in the rafts could start out immediately in hot pursuit.

As we passed the mouth of Clear Creek, Ted Quail announced that the Kaibab Suspension Bridge lay three miles ahead.

Joe signaled for the rafts to line up, twenty yards apart, and edge close to the south wall. The boatmen maneuvered left and closed up the gaps. In that configuration, Joe reasoned, their guns could be trained on the bridge from at least one raft at all times during the transit. They radioed B.J. to get Chala down.

"He won't do it," came the reply.

Joe tensed. "Why not?"

"He wants to see everything. In this narrow gorge, everything is up. He wants to *stand* up. I can't do anything with him."

Joe jumped on that. "You tell him for me to get down behind the cargo with the bodyguards around—."

Ted Quail interrupted. "There's the bridge."

All eyes turned to see the span coming into view.

"Never mind," Joe said to B.J. "Take your defensive positions. If you see the slightest movement on the bridge..."

"Not much we can do," B. J. protested. "The bridge is used by hikers."

Joe: "All right, then. If you see anyone with a *gun* aiming at your raft, *do* something about that, huh?"

B. J. said, "Roger," and went off the air.

Joe ordered all motors stopped.

In the third raft, Sam Petrie whispered to me: "Don't you think Joe's getting a little overly cautious?"

I gave him a serious look. "Better than being underly cautious, don't you think? Joe doesn't leave much to chance."

"But, Barry, we're at the bottom of a canyon five thousand feet deep, with no road around for miles. Nothing but rattlesnakes in all directions. And Joe acts as though—."

I reminded him: "He's getting ready for any emergency."

"He's getting psyched up, if you ask me."

"Sam, relax. He's doing everything I would do. There's only so far you can push Chala and high level guys like him. If they don't do as we ask..."

The bridge loomed ahead. Joe scanned it as though with laser beams, from end to end, top to bottom, all the cables, underneath, and the sheer cliff walls on either side. No one stood on the bridge. No backpacker. No gunner. He could not see a raft other than theirs, fore or aft, on the river. All remained calm. Peaceful.

The rangers on his raft had taken their positions. Joe shot a quick glance back at the other rafts. Everybody in position. Chala nowhere in sight.

Raft number one had now come within rifle range. Joe's eyes examined every foot of the span again, every parapet, wall, crevice, ledge. Ted Quail eased the raft forward beneath the left wall, controlling it with the rudder as best he could. It floated gently, soundlessly.

Indeed, not a sound filled the canyon, not even that of gurgling rapids or a canyon wren. The dark green river carried them silently, relentlessly forward in the gray morning shadows.

Joe waited and watched as the cables and deck moved directly overhead. Now Chala's raft had come into rifle range. Joe scanned the underside of the bridge again, then, on the north side of the canyon, he saw the trail to Phantom Ranch. And, for the moment at least, no sign of any human being... Maybe their worries came to nought. Maybe they had overdone the precautions to the point of—.

Suddenly, a shot rang out, echoing from wall to wall.

Joe tried to determine where it had come from, but in this natural echo chamber, the sound reverberations confused him.

His head snapped upward. He heard footsteps at the edge of the bridge, then the sound of steps on gravel. He could see nothing. His eyes darted in all directions. The echoes of gunfire faded.

Ted Quail started the motor and veered his raft sharply to the right, heading for a beach just before the rocky, bouldery outflow ridge from Bright Angel Creek. He raised his arm and signaled the other rafts to do the same.

Joe, I knew, wanted to jump into the water, scale the cliffs, and leap in pursuit up the trail. But Ted Quail took the raft to the right. And besides, by the time Joe could get out of the water and clamber up the cliff—if indeed he could, for it looked too sheer—any quarry would be long gone.

He looked at the other rafts and picked up the mike. "B.J.? You all right there?"

No answer.

In response to Quail's movement, the other boatmen started their motors and swerved their rafts to the right. The third raft maintained a thirty-yard separation. Rifle barrels poked into the air, aimed at the bridge. Nothing up there moved. No silhouette or shadow. No hiker.

"B. J.?" Joe repeated. "Is Chala all right?"

Silence.

"B. J.? Do you read?"

In moments that seemed like minutes, B. J. finally came on the air.

"Uh...we have a fatality here."

Suddenly a high-pitched call severed the silence of the inner gorge. The cheerful notes of a canyon wren came cascading from the cliffs above, pouring out in a descending scale like the tones of angelic harps.

As the first raft touched shore, Woody Watkins ordered Eddie Roff and Dalton Stubbs up the path to the bridge and on up the Kaibab Trail to see what they could find. They departed, rifles in hand.

When the other rafts landed, I looked back and scoured the cliffs with binoculars: shadowed slopes above the bridge, the trail almost hidden, the rocks black and dull pink. Nothing. What a setup. A killer's dream: shoot into the raft and be far gone before the first of the rafts could land.

The second raft landed and I jumped aboard.

"What happened?"

They carried the body of Tip, the little Thai, ashore and covered it with a tarp.

I asked B.J.: "Where was he sitting?"

B.J. pointed. "There."

I frowned. "Across from Chala?"

"Yes."

"On the other side of the raft?"

"Yes."

"Chala's all right?"

"He's gone ashore."

Buck, Evie Lund and the boatmen prepared the body for transport. Young Pete Slattery volunteered to carry it to Phantom Ranch, a short distance up the trail along Bright Angel Creek. Evie joined him.

Joe and the bodyguards, accompanied by Julie Baxter, took Chala, grim-faced and shaken, to a large rock at the edge of the creek and sat with him.

I asked the rest to assemble at the rafts.

"First of all," I asked, "what happened? Why the Thai?"

The question could not be directly answered. No one responded. I asked: "B. J., can you say what happened when you heard the shot?"

"Yes, we heard the impact of the bullet. The little guy cried out and fell forward. I judge that death was almost instantaneous."

"Where was he sitting?"

"On the floor, on the left side."

"Facing south?"

"Yes."

"And Chala?"

"We had him positioned on the opposite side, behind the cargo, on the deck. I was very concerned about going under that bridge. He resisted. As I told Joe, he said he wanted to stand up and watch as they went under. I told him we would not permit it, so he got down and I threw my protective vest over him."

"Then he could not have been seen from above?"

"Well, let's say that he could not be recognized."

"In other words, you made him look like a pile of canvas."

"Yes, sir."

I paused a moment. "That was very smart, B .J. You did exactly as you should have. That is probably what saved his life."

"Thank you, sir."

"Did you get any sense of where the shot came from?"

"South side of the bridge. No one would shoot from the north side. Too exposed."

"Okay. I have one more question for you. Why do you think the Thai got hit instead of Chala? Poor marksmanship by the killer?"

"No, sir. Very accurate marksmanship."

I raised an eyebrow. "Accurate? You mean, he *wanted* to kill Phrakonekham?"

"No sir. He wanted to kill Chala."

"Then I don't understand. Why did he shoot the Thai?"

"Because, sir, the Thai was wearing the cowboy hat."

A couple of the listeners gasped, then fell silent.

"You didn't think it would matter?"

"No, sir. Tip had been getting sunburned over the last two days. Chala tried twice to get him to wear that hat, and said 'You need it.' But Tip said 'No, you need it.' The third time, Chala just forced it on his head. I thought it was kind of odd because there wasn't too much sunlight coming down this morning. But, we'd been preaching that you can get sunstroke on a hazy day, so Chala was concerned about the Thai. Before we could do anything about it, we saw the bridge ahead and had to take our positions.

I sighed. "All right. What's done is done. We must now decide our procedure, and I want your input before we move. First, we must make arrangements regarding the body. I trust, Woody, that the park has a standard procedure for fatalities below the rim."

Woody replied: "We will call for a helicopter..."

"No!" Dee Dunn and Kent Thomas spoke almost in unison.

Woody frowned. "I beg your pardon."

Dee answered. "No helicopter."

Woody's face went blank. "I don't understand. We must get him to the rim."

Kent Thomas spoke with a determined voice. "Not by helicopter."

Woody couldn't understand. "Not by... That's our standard procedure. Why not?"

"He will not permit it."

"Who?"

"Chala."

"Our response to emergencies is the fastest possible—."

"There is no emergency, now," Dee said.

Woody insisted. "The body must be promptly removed."

"Very well, but you will not use a helicopter."

Woody shook his head. "What is the problem?"

"Chala simply will not permit it. He is adamant on that."

"Why not?"

"He is absolutely opposed to the use of helicopters in wildlife reserves. He has seen what can happen, and he won't permit it."

Woody did not respond, waiting for her to explain.

"I was with him," she went on, "in the Dominican Republic. We were taken on a helicopter trip along the east coast, scouting out a new national park. Every time we went low over a bird rookery, the birds flew out in panic, kicking eggs and young into the water, zigzagging in frantic flight. Animals are terrified. They think helicopters are ferocious hawks or eagles. The animals become panic-stricken, break their wings or necks, fall into the water, drown. He bawled out the president of the republic for that. I saw it. And ever since, he's never permitted a helicopter to be used in his presence."

A glacial look came to Woody's eyes. "Chala will not dictate what we do here. We run this park."

"Not quite," Kent Thomas said softly. "The Secretary of the Interior runs it. If you violate Chala's wishes, the Secretary of State will make certain recommendations to the Secretary of the Interior, who would then, to put it bluntly, churn your ass into mush."

Woody turned to B. J. and reached for the microphone. "Well, we'll just see about that!"

B. J. held up his hand. "I can call for horses and get the body out tomorrow. That won't be a problem."

Woody stopped, pondered, pouted....and acquiesced. "All right. I will accompany the body to the rim. Designate a ranger to go with me."

B. J. turned away.

I turned to Dietrich. "What about deposition of the remains?"

Dietrich thought for a moment. "He was a Buddhist. I will instruct your people on the rim about whom to call regarding his records. He was a State Department interpreter. They assigned him to Chala because he knew some African dialects as well as French. His file will state what he wanted done in case of...this." His voice took on an acid tone. "What a pity he couldn't have been protected properly."

I ignored that remark. "Very well. If you'll get together with Woody on that, please. Right after lunch. Now we have another immediate problem. Where do we go from here?

Joe and Julie joined the group.

"We've just had a long conversation with Chala," he said.

"How's he taking this?" I asked.

"For someone concerned with all life, he's taking it pretty hard. He blames himself for everything."

I asked: "Why?"

"Because he let Tip borrow that hat. In fact, pushed it on his head. Without thinking. Just wanted to keep the little guy from getting sunburned."

"We can't let him assume guilt here."

Joe nodded. "I know. I worked on him. Julie worked on him. She's the one who really talked him out of it. She told him about a killer up there somewhere in the cliffs, the hatred of people, the love of killing, all universal. He snapped out of the initial gloom, but he's still *desolé,* as he puts it."

"Was he close to the Thai? Had they been friends a long time?"

"No. Hadn't met before this trip. But he's upset."

"Well, I imagine we all are. Did you discuss what he wants to do now?"

"He wants to go on."

"You're sure?"

"Positive. He said Tip was so polite and considerate. He would feel terrible, wherever he is, if he thought that we abandoned the trip on his account."

"Then you're positive Chala wants to go through with the rest of the trip? As planned. Did he understand?"

"We talked with him in detail. There's no doubt about it."

"There may be more danger. This may be a band of killers. They'll still stalk him if they find out the wrong guy was killed."

"I explained all that. He said, 'So? We have to assume so, no matter what.' He doesn't care. He's lived with this all of his adult life. In these recent years, he's always been in danger. He's gotten so it doesn't bother him. He trusts the rangers. He loves them because they protect wildlife. It's that simple."

I was still not satisfied. "How does he feel? How is he physically?"

"Upset, of course. But he's strong. He'll be all right after lunch."

Ted Quail asked, "Then we'll get lunch now? If we're going on to camp tonight, we have to make up for lost time."

I nodded. The crew took from the rafts the tables, chests and kegs, and started setting them up on shore.

When they had gone, I stood in front of the group and pondered for a moment. I glanced over at Chala, sitting with the bodyguards, head in hands. Julie broke the silence.

"He does have one request. He wants his blue robes."

I turned toward her. "What for?"

"He wants to say goodbye to his friend. He believes that the little Thai is on his way back to the cosmos from which he came. He thinks we should all say goodbye and thank the little guy for being so kind as to join us and help us on earth."

I nodded. "By all means. I will handle that. Do you think that right after lunch would be suitable?"

"Yes," she answered.

"And Woody, I think you're right to accompany the Thai to the rim as an honor guard. Ritual is everything. The ranking officer present—yourself—and a ranger. You're arranging that?"

Watkins nodded.

I turned to the group. "All right. Chala wants to go on. Do all the rest of you want to go ahead? Is there anyone, disturbed enough by what has happened, who wishes to go out of the canyon at this point? You are free to leave, and there will certainly be no objection on my part."

No response.

"I didn't think anyone would leave, but I wanted it on record that you had the chance, without prejudice. So...we will go on. But it will not be any less risky. We don't know whether this has been done by an individual or by a team of killers. We shall assume that a team is stalking us. If so, they'll try again. They are likely ahead of us. They may be strung out along the canyon, perhaps intending to go after other members of Chala's staff. I don't mean to alarm you unduly, but I want you to be more alert than ever. Our goal is still to give Chala maximum protection. You have any problems with that, Woody?"

"If one of the rangers and I stay behind to take the corpse up to the rim," Woody replied, "you'll be short-handed."

"That can be handled."

"And you still want horses when you get to Supai?"

"At the village. As planned."

Woody looked around. "Then I see no problem, if no one else does."

The crew got out food and set up the kegs of drinks.

"I have one other current problem," I said. "We must find out who did this."

"I've already started," said Woody. "My plan is to alert Lee Federico to have a ranger at the top of the Kaibab Trail to apprehend the killer when he climbs out."

"Can they identify him?"

"Anyone coming out of the canyon with a rifle will be apprehended."

"He might hide or discard his weapon."

"Possible."

"Or come out at night."

Woody: "True. I don't say we can get him. I just want the rangers alerted."

"Okay," I responded, "if you can possibly spare the men, you might also want to cover the top of the Bright Angel Trail."

"We will."

I noticed Buck Stevens staring at me in an odd, serious way. As I watched, the river ranger moved his eyes in the direction of Phantom Ranch. I comprehended.

"There is one other aspect I want to pursue. I'd like to investigate the situation at this end."

"Here?" Woody asked, surprised.

"Yes."

"There isn't much time. The rafts must leave after lunch in order to get to the next camp site." I called to Ted Quail. "Ted, how long to camp tonight?"

"We have to leave as soon as possible after lunch. We're off schedule now. We can't run this river after dark. Besides, the biggest rapids are just ahead."

Woody turned back to me. "There. You don't have much time."

I answered promptly. "I know that. I'm staying behind."

This statement turned into something of a bombshell for the entire group.

"You're *what?*" asked Dietrich.

"Barry!" said Sam Petrie, astonished. "You're in charge."

I answered. "Joe's in charge for the rest of your trip."

Kent Thomas asked: "What can you do here?"

Dee Dunn: "What if we need you farther on?"

B. J.: "You'll need help?"

I answered promptly. "Yes, I will. I'd like Buck to stay here, too"

That remark hit them like a second bombshell.

Dietrich's voice became strident. "He's the river ranger! You can't take him away from us! How will we get on?"

Buck answered quietly. "The boatmen know this river better than I do."

"I don't care! Barry, you agreed to conduct us through...I mean... We—."

Woody objected. "That leaves the group undermanned by two more people."

I nodded. "I've thought of that,"

Julie said: "You're on to something."

"Yes," I said. "I am on to something. I need someone who knows the canyon."

Neff Neilson said: "No one knows it like Buck."

"Exactly," I said.

"You won't be able to catch up with us," said B. J.

I agreed. "I don't intend to. We'll be in touch."

Questions poured out.

"What's up? You have some clues?"

"Something we don't know?"

"Where'll you go?"

"What will you do?"

"At this point," I responded, slowly and deliberately, "I haven't the slightest idea."

Eddie Roff and Dalton Stubbs returned during lunch. They had climbed to the top of the Inner Gorge and looked out over the lower plateau. They heard nothing and saw nothing, except some young backpackers. Nothing suspicious. They had run part of the way back down. Perspiration soaked their clothing.

After lunch, Chala donned his blue robes and assembled the group for a short ceremony. Nothing, I thought, could have seemed in such worldly contrast, as though in a dream. Here, among the red rocks and black cliffs rose a human figure in sky blue robes. A simple human figure with bare black head and deep black eyes. An imposing prince of the forest... dwarfed by the canyon walls.

As Chala spoke, neither Joe nor I translated because we did not want our voices inserted into so solemn an occasion. We listened, enraptured, however, to the liquid words and phrases. To the rich adulation for a public person who learned so much and served his friends so well. Who gave his life in the noblest duties of man—the search for knowledge, and the saving of life.

Now he turns to ashes, Chala said. Now he joins the cosmic dust from which he rose. We can but thank him humbly. Rejoice that he came to us. Rejoice that he lived with us on earth for as long as he did. Rejoice that he left with honor...

After a moment of silence, he said, with feeling: "Bon voyage, ami de l'univers..."

Nobody spoke for a minute. Chala then returned to his rock, removed the blue robe, and prepared for departure.

I was prepared to offer a few comments in English, but desisted. Nothing else need be offered.

Nobody spoke as they put on life jackets and took their seats. But the solemnity did not last long. Chala, not one to mope, dispelled it.

"Joseph, ami, allons-y!" he shouted, laughing and waving the cowboy hat.

Joe rose to the occasion, waving his park ranger cap. "Let's go!"

"Aux cataractes! Les chutes d'eau! Les plus violents, le mieux!"

"To the rapids!" Joe translated. "The more violent the better! Allons! Let's go!"

Caught in the mood, relieved of tension, the rest of the passengers broke the somber spell, lifted their hats to Chala, and shouted: "Allons!"

As soon as they boarded, the crews untied the ropes, and the rafts moved out into the water. They floated away in order, Joe standing in the first raft, and headed downstream, the passengers waving at their comrades remaining behind. As they disappeared around the bend, Woody turned away from the river and started toward Phantom Ranch.

"I have to call the rim," he said to Buck and me. "You two coming to the ranch?"

I demurred. "Thanks, Woody. I think I'll come up later."

Woody left. I strolled down to the water's edge, Buck following, and for a long time studied the bridge, the river, the trail up the slopes, the trail on the opposite bank of the river.

Buck said nothing at first, then quietly: "Unless I miss my guess, you are thinking the same thing I am."

I said, "This may be entirely wrong, Buck. But something about this whole thing doesn't quite add up. And if I'm right...if it *doesn't* add up... then this is a pretty astonishing matter."

Buck reflected on those words and then said: "Go on."

I sat on a red sandstone boulder that had rolled with the floods down Bright Angel Creek. "Suppose I were a killer," I said. "Suppose I'm a smart killer. And suppose I shot someone from the far end of that bridge."

"Yes?"

"I would assume there were rangers swarming all over the place. In this particular instance, all along the river banks. And, of course, up on the rims."

I paused in thought, examining the scene again from rim to river. "I would assume that it would be foolish to climb to either rim. Certainly not on the regular trails. Would you follow that line of reasoning?"

"Sounds logical. Go on."

"Then, barring those routes of escape, I would search for another trail. One less traveled. One with more hiding places. One not far away from the scene of the crime. Or, conceivably, another way to the rim. Are there trails to the rim other than Kaibab and Bright Angel?"

"Yes. They're some distance from here. You need to know the country pretty well. Maybe have some trail maps, booklets, route descriptions. A smart killer would have them, do you think?"

"I would. Are they good trails?"

Buck answered slowly. "Most are not maintained. Some are falling into pretty serious disrepair. Hazardous, we say.

Not recommended for hiking. And certainly not for anyone to hike alone."

"Then our killer could leave the canyon by one of those old trails, even though it would be a long way around?"

"Conceivably."

"Less congested? That would be to his advantage."

"Yes."

I thought for a moment. "Now, what about the possibility of climbing out of the canyon at night?"

"Possible. On the regular trails you can see your way, even without moonlight. But on these nonmaintained trails, there could be possible missteps..."

I nodded. "Understood. Altogether, then, it would probably be best not to go out of the canyon at all. Not on a regular trail. Not on one of the old trails. Do you buy that?"

"Barry, I'm with you, I think. You mean, not go out at least for a while?"

"You're following, Buck. Not go anywhere until this thing fades? Maybe stay down here somewhere for a few weeks. Does that make sense to you?"

"Yes."

"Well, then, the next question is obvious. How many good hiding places are there down here?"

"Two or three million."

"Good. Which one would you pick?"

Buck grinned. "Barry, I am now way ahead of you."

Meanwhile, the rest of the party, under Joe's direction, and with Ted Quail guiding the rafts, continued its descent down the Colorado.

The rafts headed for what Rudy Vogel called "The Big Three:" Granite, Hermit and Crystal rapids.

"Toughest of the bunch," he said. "Hang on with everything you got!"

At Granite rapids, the water crashed along a black wall on the north side of the river. Each raft, in its turn, whipped and yawed among the giant waves, like a stricken vessel trying to land on a turbulent seacoast. With almost explosive force, waves leaped higher than the raft, which one moment headed to midriver, the next toward the cliffs. The nose soared up, the pontoons rearing like headless horses in the maelstrom.

With white waves surging all around it, each raft seemed diminished in this sea of flying water. It rose and tipped toward the cliff, as though to dash to pieces like each foaming crest, but then fell back and veered away.

Once again, Joe got the worst of it. Seated in front, he went down into each trough to meet the crest of succeeding waves. Soaring fountains deluged the passengers again and again. The rafts climbed hillocks of roiling river, free above the flood, only to dive into valleys of rippling foam beyond.

At one point, Joe saw a wave ahead shooting up twelve feet. He ducked. Down it came. The passengers disappeared. Only the boatman stood above, hand on rudder.

Lurching and jerking, leaping and plunging, the rafts pummeled the passengers as they gripped the cargo ropes. In this thundering world, their legs went flying upwards as the vessel fell out from under them, dropped back as the raft crashed again into another chaotic liquid canyon.

And then the violence subsided as the waves diminished.

"That's enough!" howled Joe in mock terror. "We can't go on like this!"

But they did. A mile farther on they glided at high speed into the roller coaster of Hermit rapids. Here, in a long, straight course, the river became giant ripples—long waves and troughs that threw each raft high and pulled it down at high speed. Like no other roller coaster he'd been on, Joe thought. At the top, the raft seemed to skid on its tail before diving forward and down with a crash.

Not a member of each raft's passenger contingent failed to seize the thrill of it. After all, how many times at home (or anywhere?) had they been so vigorously tossed from side to side and stem to stern? Hurled in what seemed like uncontrolled abandon down a roaring river in a canyon of rocks painted every shade of red?

They accompanied their wild ride with shrieks and hoots, which often got truncated by a sudden dousing.

Dee Dunn and Kent Thomas, normally most reticent of the group, lost all pretense of conservatism, shouting with everyone else. Chala whooped the most. Dietrich Deitemeyer banged the rubber pontoon in elation. Sam Petrie said he had not "whooped and hollered" like this in years. The river

transported them back into those forgotten years when youth amounted almost to daily abandon. For a while, at least, they could forget the sadness of little Tip. They could become very small human beings in a very large canyon and very wild world.

"I'd pay a fortune for this!" Sam shouted, half sputtering.

"That's what it's worth," Dee shouted back.

The canyon walls flew by in a blur. So did time. Minutes became seconds and then disappeared entirely. The passengers lost track of time in this forward momentum. Nothing mattered in this untamed world. Nothing but rocks and water and high speed.

And in another three miles they came to Crystal.

"Ai-yee-ee!" Joe shrieked again.

This time the rafts headed straight for a wall of pink boulders rolled out from Crystal Creek. That pushed the mighty river once again into a narrow curving chute to the left, condensed its fury into an arc of violence. As the water surged in that direction, it rammed into ledges of the opposite wall with thundering impact. Then waves and dancing fountains dashed down the river for as far as the eye could see.

Joe watched foam waves shooting up ten feet, and giant ripples from which, he thought, there could be no escape.

"Surely we're not going down into *that!*" he called to Ted Quail.

The boatman smiled calmly and said in a vigorous tone: "Brace, buddy, brace!"

Perched on the lip of the rapid, Joe got a panoramic, unobstructed view. They headed directly for the pile of rocks that blocked half the river. If they hit at this speed, it would somersault them, boat and all, over the boulder dam into the roaring waves beyond. Pitch out the passengers. Hurl them into the whirlpools. How would he react? Swim for dear life. After all, he had on a life jacket. Float downstream until the water calmed. Then move over to the shore and—*stop it!* He cursed himself. "Stop it! Nightmares you don't need!"

The boat, like the current, abruptly swerved to the left...and headed for the opposite wall. Just before hitting, it swerved again. The current tossed the boat around the end of the bouldery dam—the rocks just off the starboard bow. The force then sent the raft careening into the downstream turbulence, thrusting it about like a chip on the open sea. They veered over to the right side of the river beneath a black cliff that fell steeply into the water.

Joe looked back quickly, facetiously, to see whether Quail had fallen asleep. Not so! He had as tight a grip on the rudder as ever.

The other rafts sailed wildly down the chute. More shrieks and laughter echoed among the cliffs.

The waves became tamer, but the water still rolled the raft from side to side beneath rugged cliffs of pinkish granite and the glistening black of schist.

Crystal would not be their last rapid, but no other exceeded it in fury. "Except Lava Falls," Rudy Vogel told Joe later. "Lava's the grandaddy of 'em all. Sorry you ain't gonna see it. We leave the river at Havasu."

"Aw, shucks!" Joe said. *The river does that to you,* he thought. *Makes you wish you could go on crashing through rapids for days and days and days...*

They made steady progress during the afternoon. The boatmen allowed no free floating now. They had to make up time lost at Bright Angel Creek. Hence, the motors drove them steadily forward.

To Joe, the rapids that followed went by as though in a dream... Sapphire, Turquoise, Serpentine...wetting and rewetting them so often that they came to pay little attention to it. They passed the hundred-mile mark. Joe reflected that their departure from Lee's Ferry seemed at once only yesterday and at the same time a year ago. Among these cliffs and placid pools he felt he could spend another year, climbing, exploring, contemplating. Yet in a year, he knew, he would not see anything twice. Nor even a fraction of what exists.

Bass rapids, Shinumo, Hundred-and-ten Mile, Hakatai, Waltenberg. The passengers chattered like children, mesmerized by soaring canyon walls and amphitheaters that dwarfed them into insignificance.

Suddenly, Ted Quail turned off the motor, and they drifted to a rocky shore. "Elves Chasm," he announced.

They climbed the rocks to a series of stairstep cascades, tranquil pools, moss covered rocks, and patches of fern.

On the way back, they felt better. They had touched reality again. A calm and steady world without crashing waves or furious whirlpools. The green of the ponds, the red of the giant walls above, helped ease from their hearts the pain of the murder. It didn't matter now. The little Thai had gone to a paradise of his own. They would live in theirs.

They arrived at their rocky, sandy, camp site in Stephen Aisle as the orange sun washed the walls with evening glow and turned the river from green to gold. The gorge remained as it had since noon, a furnace, the walls giving back high heat absorbed in the long summer day ...

Chala said little. Instead of his usual effervescent self he seemed morose. Joe tried to comfort him, but with little success. Joe knew how painful it must be to go on without his companion and interpreter.

Buck and I, having remained behind at Phantom Ranch, filled our backpacks with water, rations and bedding, and left as the last dregs of daylight turned the pink granite walls to somber gray.

The trail led north, at first beneath giant cottonwoods that towered like haunting black ghosts into what little sky lay above this narrow canyon. Then we walked through sparse scrub.

Before long, we came to a junction. A trail to the right bent back and climbed up the slope.

"Trail to Clear Creek," Buck said. "Here's where we stake out." He pointed in the direction they had been traveling. "The North Kaibab Trail goes on up Bright Angel Creek to the North Rim—very well traveled. If our killer shows up here and goes that way, we know he'll be heading for the North Rim. That would be rather stupid of him."

"Why?"

"Because you can't very easily sneak up on to the rim. Rangers are waiting. He's not going to get past them."

"There must be a car somewhere. If this guy drove to Lee's Ferry and came down the river, he would have to get back to Lee's Ferry to pick up his car."

Buck: "Maybe. My guess is that he had accomplices."

"Why?"

"This is a complex operation. They may have used the South Rim as a base, planned things carefully, and decided on holing up down here after making their kill. Bring down supplies, hide out, and wait."

I watched the stars appearing in the narrow sky overhead. "That would take planning. And money. And at least three people. Any guesses?"

"Pretty clear cut."

"Who?"

"Babb Brothers."

"The Goons we met at the river junction? I had the same idea. The question is, where are they now?"

Buck kept his eye on the trail. "I've known of them for some time. Always getting into some kind of trouble in Flagstaff, Kanab, Kingman. They get hired where there's dirty work to do. They're a natural for this. And if anyone talks about taking their guns away, that would rile them up like nothing else."

"They're after Chala?"

"I haven't figured it all out yet."

Curious, I said: "We've only seen them once. At the Little Colorado junction. They were supposed to leave when they got to Phantom Ranch."

"Well, I doubt if they did. There are two tricks here. One is that they never walk if they don't have to. So they must have some horses somewhere. And the second is that there are *four* Babb Brothers."

"Four? You're sure?"

Buck nodded. "I've met them. Usually, they stick together. You seldom hear of them doing any jobs separately."

"Okay," I mused. "that could change the picture a little. Tie some threads together. That would account for the three we saw—they came down the river and landed at Bright Angel Creek. One got off to kill Chala but got the Thai instead. Only he probably doesn't know that since he didn't stick around to find out what happened. Hides out for the day, afraid to be seen, afraid to go to the rim."

"What about the others?" I asked.

"The other Goons can't go to Phantom Ranch or either rim. They have to get off the river, too. They know we're right behind them and would recognize their pink raft."

"Right. So?"

Buck thought for a moment. "So they go on. They'll set up somewhere else down the Colorado. Trouble is, we don't know where. In case Goon One didn't finish off Chala, they'll have another chance. Does this sound like them?"

"No. I can't conceive of them doing anything that intelligent."

Buck grinned. "Nevertheless, Joe could be leading Chala into another trap."

"Probably. He's ready for that." I waited a moment, then went on. "Suppose the Babb Brothers aren't smart. Suppose they're dumb. As dumb as you say they are."

Buck said: "Okay. But if you do that, you'll probably have to revise some of your theories."

I had already revised them, and told him so. I had been revising them since yesterday. "Someone else has to be bossing the operation. If what I think is true, the Babb Brothers are more than just determined to get Chala. There's more of a motive than just knocking off a guy because he has a dangerous proposal. They are not that motivated."

Buck gave a slow, low laugh. "I'm with you."

I went on. "Then there's the fourth brother. If he's down here, and the raft with the other two Goons has gone on

downstream, there's no escape out of the canyon. The killer and the fourth Goon have to *stay* down here."

Buck said, softly: "That sounds like somebody else's planning. But they could still be alone in this."

"Granted. Has the fourth brother gotten down here ahead of time? Brought horses? Supplies?"

"Possible."

"And set up camp?"

"Yes. Could be."

"So? They'd need water."

"That's why we're here," Buck answered. "It would have to be Clear Creek if anywhere. Away from the mainstream of hikers. We've ruled out everywhere else."

"How far is it?"

"Nearly nine miles."

"Can you get down to the Colorado from there?"

"Yes, and when we passed the junction I scanned very carefully. They could have shot from the mouth of Clear Creek. Unlikely, though. One of us could have jumped in, gone ashore, and chased them upstream."

"All right. None of this we *know*."

Buck thought quietly in the darkness, and finally said: "True. So we wait. But if we don't have it right, there's going to be a lot of mud on your face."

I replied: "Both our faces."

"I'm innocent. You asked me to go with you."

Buck led the way to a small outcrop of rocks behind which we could conceal ourselves. We put down our packs and surveyed the scene. The stars overhead had become brilliant, but began to fade as the moon rose. I felt relieved at the prospect of a little additional lighting, even though the moon had begun to wane. Buck probably had little need for light. He knew the outlines of the inner canyon. He had become attuned to the tiny noises, the crickets, the cicadas, and his experience enabled him to distinguish and identify noises and objects that would seem unfamiliar to anyone else.

Far up on the rim, seven miles in a straight line, I saw an occasional flash of light, some auto on a highway along the rim, probably. As the evening wore on, these lights diminished in frequency. The quiet and solitude became almost complete.

I liked Buck's reasoning. I liked mine, too, even though it called for a considerable leap of faith and the accuracy of certain premises. Still, I had problems with some of this. If indeed the Goons had conspired to wipe out Chala, how did they find out about his visit? They didn't seem like types who regularly read newspapers. Or read anything.

Had word-of-mouth reached them? Had the world of hunters been buzzing with this news? If so, how far in advance? Getting ready for this kind of stalking crime required at least some basic preparations. And some basic money, too.

From what Buck had said—their taking odd jobs, dirty jobs—he couldn't quite conclude that they had the resources to mount this complex an expedition.

The timing, I said to myself. *The timing is everything. How did the Goons know when to set their pink float into the Colorado at Lee's Ferry? And where did they learn to navigate a river so tricky, so dangerous to amateurs? Above all, where had they learned about Chala?*

I wanted to question Buck some more... Not now. If the Goon or Goons left their hiding place at midnight, came down to one of the suspension bridges, and crossed the Colorado, they should be getting near. I looked at the faint luminous dial of my watch. Almost one.

I listened for the hooves of horses coming down the Clear Creek trail to meet someone... Nothing. The silence overwhelmed us. Not even an owl hooted. No coyote called. No nighthawk dived with whirring wings. Nothing...

Suddenly, Buck tapped my shoulder.

We heard the sound of footsteps. Faint, but unmistakable.

Moments later, a dim shadow moved up the trail from Phantom Ranch.

Had Buck been right? Guessed the actions of the Goons?

Well, I asked myself, who else *could* it be at this hour?

Easy. Some night hikers. They do that in this blistering canyon during the summer. They would want to stop and chat with us.

Buck had an uncanny knack about predicting what people in this part of the country would do. I began to feel elated—though we still had to verify the identity of this hiker in the night.

The figure arrived at the junction about fifty yards from where we sat. He paused. Suddenly, he switched on a small flashlight, looked around for a moment, then switched it off again. The sudden luminance of the tiny light seemed like a searchlight in the darkness.

What monumental indiscretion! I thought. The guy obviously didn't imagine that anyone else could be in this canyon after midnight, much less watching from fifty paces away.

All one of us had to do now was sneeze to screw up the whole effort.

He seemed to pause in uncertainty. Which way to go? He obviously hadn't been here before. Maybe there was no plan. Or maybe it was too dark for anyone to be certain.

If he went on up the Kaibab Trail toward the North rim, Buck's scenario would be shattered...

The figure hesitated, looked around. From our position, we could make out no features, scarcely even a profile—nothing with which to attempt an identification.

I held my breath.

After another minute of apparent indecision, the shadow turned and began to climb the trail to Clear Creek.

What a relief!

So far, so good.

But we waited. Were there others? Anyone following? An accomplice?

We waited. The silence grew heavy again as the sounds of footsteps faded. The figure disappeared in the darkness, but we could see him flashing the light from time to time as he went up the trail.

I waited for Buck to make the first move. We had to allow our quarry a good head start. In canyons whose walls reflect the slightest sounds, we had to let distance muffle our pursuit. In air so clear, where sounds travel long distances with ease, we could not give our quarry the slightest audible clue that anyone pursued him.

If that happened, he would hide and wait for us...

And what about any other Goons? Had they gone up the South Kaibab Trail to the South Rim after all? Instead of down the river? Had Buck misjudged them?

Buck doubtless pondered similar questions as we waited. We sat stock still. There might be an accomplice following.

Moreover, the Goon gone by could be presumed to stop occasionally up the trail to see if anyone followed. In due course, the flashing light grew smaller and disappeared.

Ten minutes more, and nothing happened. No moving shadows. No following footsteps. No calls. And now, no light at all on the trail above.

Another ten minutes passed. How long would Buck delay?

I prepared to rise. He held back. No one knew this canyon better than Buck, or had an ear better tuned to its sounds.

My mind spun in the darkness, trying to connect odd events of the last three days. And with that I began to sort out certain suspicions...to put two and two together...

Buck rose, lifted his backpack and put it on. I did likewise. We paused again, listening.

No owl. No coyote. Only crickets.

We left our hiding place and started up the trail to Clear Creek.

We climbed in the faint light of the moon, able to see where to place each step, not needing the glare of a flashlight. I glanced at my watch. Two a.m.

The long climb eastward out of Bright Angel Canyon—slowed because of our deliberate attempt to maintain silence—took nearly an hour. Always above loomed the layered cliffs of the Tapeats sandstone, shadowed like a black wall of doom, whose goblins could break out at any moment and suffocate us into oblivion.

What incongruities! I thought. A colorful canyon now dark and colorless. A canyon of life now tainted with death. The pursuit of joy now a pursuit of evil.

One happy change. The brutal temperatures of day had moderated in the breezes of night. Up here, the heat radiating from canyon walls had a chance to escape. But we hiked uphill, perspiring. The slow climb with backpacks became grueling.

After what seemed to me at least two miles, we broke out onto the Tonto Plateau beneath Sumner Butte, which

towered eerily in the waxlike light of the waning moon. Below lay the awesome abyss of the Inner Gorge, nearly a thousand feet deep. Down there, in the black, flowed the Colorado River...invisible...inaudible.

We stopped, set down our packs, and listened. A pinpoint of light appeared, ahead along the trail. We reached into our packs for binoculars.

The light illuminated the profile of a horse. Then a rider. Then another horse. The figure with the flashlight grasped the saddle horn and pulled himself up, the light beam shooting in all directions.

We heard a human voice, a sharp bark, and the light went out. Then more talking, so faint that we could not distinguish the words. Then the clatter of hooves. And as the minutes passed the sounds grew fainter.

For the first time since the trail junction, Buck spoke...in a low and guarded voice. "Somebody brought a horse to pick up the son-of-a-bitch. How the hell did he know to do that?"

"Prearranged plan?" I offered.

"Okay," Buck said, "but how could he have known whether the guy would be there?"

"Well, they must have some kind of communication."

"Maybe. He must have learned that the killing did occur."

"Not necessarily, Buck. If the guy with the horses was sitting over in Clear Creek, nine miles away, it's a little far-fetched to think he got all the news..."

"Well, then, it was luck. Coincidence."

I gave a negative harrumph. "I don't believe in luck. Or coincidence, either."

We hung the binoculars around our necks and hoisted our backpacks.

"Now what?" I asked.

"Now we go get the bastards!" Buck answered.

We resumed our passage along the trail, less careful now, knowing our quarry moved amid the clatter of horses' hooves. Buck kept the lead and I followed him as though following a dark gray amorphous cloud.

The moon went behind a cliff, and the dark rocks on a dark trail made footing more treacherous. We maintained maximum alert. If our quarry stopped for whatever reason, we could come upon them suddenly in a blaze of gunfire. For that reason, Buck stopped now and then to listen. Sometimes we heard the faint sound of horses' hooves. Sometimes we didn't—the riders either stopped and listening ... or on the far side of a talus slope.

The night hike bore into my brain like an auger. At times I felt tired—at times numbed as the trail curved repeatedly, almost monotonously, around natural talus—rocky slopes that never seemed to straighten out. Buck had insisted we nap the previous afternoon at Phantom, readying ourselves for a

long night. That helped, but the rhythm of footsteps, hour after hour, dulled my senses.

The death of the little Thai seemed distant now, and distorted, like something out of delirium tremens, a remote nightmare that floated in a void without reality. Yet the reality—that I had let it happen—bothered me. I tried and tried to figure out how I could have stopped it. That taunted and eluded me. Maybe I couldn't have. Maybe no one could have. But it happened on my watch. I should have seen something, anything, to head that off and save the little Thai's life. If I could have avoided it, I would have never gone under that bridge. I had only one consolation. Chala still lived.

I wondered where Joe and the rest of the group had camped. Whether they had gotten through the roughest rapids without trouble. Whether they had climbed to Elves Chasm. Where the other Goons had gone. I mulled over the puzzle again and again, the missing pieces of the Goons and the murder.

At length, my mind refused to access any image but the shadow of the walking figure ahead and the faint configurations of the rocks on the trail beneath my feet.

Bend after bend after bend in the trail...repetitious, mesmerizing, unending. The moon had almost set behind the western rim.

After what seemed like an eternity of hiking, I chanced to look up. Beyond the far eastern rim, the sky had become noticeably lighter. The distant rims and high stone "temples" towering toward the stars showed the faintest of silhouettes.

Dawn had begun. Dawn of the day when, as Buck had said, "we go get the bastards."

"Transportation. Miss Barcroft."

"Edie, this is Maureen at Phantom. How are you this morning?"

"Oh, Maureen, fine, thank you. I was just about to call you. How are things down there? Hot?"

"Not yet. But it will be. Now the reason I called you, Edie ..."

"I know, Maureen."

"We still have a corpse down here."

"Yes, you sure do, and I told you yesterday we'd have a wrangler and three horses down there by nightfall."

"Well, they didn't get here, Edie."

"I know they didn't. I tried and tried..."

"Now we have a very irate assistant superintendent down here."

"I'm sorry, Maureen, but after I talked to you, I couldn't find a wrangler anywhere. And every last mule and horse is out, except the lame ones."

"Out? Where are they all?"

"We had forty-six people on the afternoon rim ride yesterday."

"That many?"

"Yes. So that left nothing—not even a donkey—in the corrals. I called the chief ranger's office and told them. They said that on such sudden notice there wasn't anything they could do. Maureen, I've never seen a demand like this... We just get more tourists every year!"

"Tell me about it, Edie. I can sure understand. Really. So what about today? Mister Watkins is steaming."

"That's what I was going to call you about. I got hold of Rusty Gorman and he thinks he can break away, if he can get help from the park stables. They're all out on trail repair jobs, though."

"Then what are we going to do? The corpse..."

"Well, Maureen, I think we're in luck. I just got a couple of cancellations. I can give Rusty two horses—."

"We need three. Watkins and a ranger will be accompanying the body. It's a kind of diplomatic thing, you know? Like real urgent."

"Well, for Heaven's sake, why don't they use 'copters like they usually do?"

"It's strange. They got some reason."

"Well, isn't this an emergency?"

"I guess not. The guy is dead. All I know is they need three horses, and it has got to be today. Without fail. Watkins says so. And you know, Edie, he supervises concessions in the park..."

"Yes, I do know that."

"And he's mad."

"I know that, too. All right, Maureen. I'll get another horse if I have to make one. They'll come down Kaibab and be there by supper time."

"No earlier?"

"Rusty's got a morning ride. Can't get away till noon. And anyway, it doesn't matter. He can't start back up till tomorrow morning. Has to have a good night's rest, feed the horses, and so on."

"Okay, Edie, you did your best. I appreciate all your help. How's the weather up there?"

"Maureen, you don't want to know!"

"You're right, Edie. Talk to you later."

"Cheers."

The rafts arrived at Deer Creek Falls, a sparkling freshwater oasis at the edge of the Colorado River, with the passengers, especially the rangers, in high dudgeon about Chala. Anyone so notorious as to be the target of assassins had to be *somebody*. Anyone who had been chased and shot at would get anyone's attention. He rankled others to the point of murder. Yet he remained a mystical ghost. They couldn't communicate. They couldn't reach him.

"What do we know?" asked Dalton Stubbs. "Practically nothing."

"So why should you know?" asked Cynthia Kasbolt.

"Because we're risking our lives to protect him, that's why."

"That's not all for me," she added. "I think he's also an interesting guy."

"You got to admit," said Angel, "he's widening a lot of horizons."

As the crew set up a table on a rock shelf beside the river, and started preparing lunch, the queries turned to Kathi LeClair.

"You interviewed him," Stubbs said. "We know his background. Africa. Animal lover. All that. But I still can't figure out what he's *really* after?"

"Yes," added Mozo Fernandez, "we can sympathize. But just the same, we've come all this way and hardly know who he is."

"Or what he's really trying to do," added Eddie Roff. "All we want to know is, who *is* this guy?"

Kathi petitioned Joe to set up another interview especially for the rangers, with all the passengers listening in, and Joe translating.

No sooner said than done. They collected their sandwiches, accompanied by Ted Quail's muttering: "I don't give a damn what he says, he ain't going to take my gun away from me."

They gathered, crew and all, on a grassy space beside the river.

To Joe, once again, the exchange seemed to play like dramatic theater.

KATHI. Your eminence, everybody is curious. We've heard some of your ideas. But not everybody understands. A lot of these people think you want to take their guns away.

CHALA. *(Hands thrown up.)* O ma foi! I don't want *anybody's* guns.

KATHI. But you want the shooting stopped.

CHALA. I never said I wanted shooting stopped.

KATHI. Well, then, what *do* you want?

CHALA. I want people to stop killing wild animals. By shooting, traps, snares, whatever.

KATHI. That's all?

CHALA. That's all!

KATHI. You don't care about cows, chickens, laboratory rats, zoos?

CHALA. Yes. But it's not for me. Let somebody else handle that.

KATHI. You're solely concerned with animals in the wild?

CHALA. Yes.

KATHI. You're worried about them disappearing?

CHALA. Yes. Does that surprise anyone?

KATHI. I shouldn't think so.

CHALA. Is that difficult to understand?

KATHI. Well, not here in a national park. But why your crusade?

CHALA. *(Sweep of hands.)* Like I said, wild animals are disappearing. Everywhere.

KATHI. What reasons do you give for this?

CHALA. People. Too many people. Greedy people. Killing them. Poaching them. Crowding them out. Too many cities. They're destroying animal habitat.

KATHI. Is it that bad?

CHALA. Look at your own seacoasts in North America. Off Canada, New England, Washington. They have fished out the cod, tuna, salmon. Those fish are almost gone. But they could turn it around.

KATHI. Greedy people?

CHALA. Stupid people. Overfishing. No conservation. Now the fishermen have no work. No jobs. And they blame it on seals. Seals! How stupid! Seals keep fish populations *healthy!* Any ecologist knows that.

KATHI. Okay. It's bad.

CHALA. Halibut. Did you know? Commercial halibut fishing is now limited to *one day a year!*

KATHI. I didn't know that. More greedy people?

CHALA. Hungry people. Yes, yes, of course. Not enough fish. What are we doing to ourselves?

KATHI. They say we have to have jobs...

CHALA. *Fichtre!* Le diable avec cela! They've taken all the fish. That's why there are no jobs. Are tigers next? Pandas? Deer?

KATHI. Then we should get rid of people?

CHALA. Yes! They are not an endangered species.

KATHI. (*Taken aback.*) You mean really reduce human populations?

CHALA. (*Forthrightly.*) I certainly do.

KATHI. Fewer greedy people?

CHALA. Yes.

KATHI. Fewer people hunting wildlife?

CHALA. Yes.

KATHI. This could be considered a radical idea.

CHALA. Not by animals.

KATHI. Are these the policies of the UN Environment Programme?

CHALA. You asked for *my* ideas. Forget UNEP.

KATHI. Then you would advocate the removal of human beings?

CHALA. To lower the human population pressure against wild animals. Yes. Of course! Is that too difficult to understand? We *must* do it.

KATHI. (*Searching for words.*) Well, then, uh, would you set up systems for...er...eliminating human beings?

CHALA. That's not necessary... Such systems already exist.

KATHI. They do?

CHALA. Certainly. War, famine, disease, smoking, drinking, overeating, speeding, suicide. All voluntary. All natural. We need more of these.

(*General commotion in audience.*)

QUAIL. (*Angrily.*) I told you this guy was a nut. A pure nut.

NEILSON. Well, technically, I suppose he has a point. Most animals have a self-destruct system when they overpopulate. Lemmings, for one.

CHALA. *Voilá!* Instead of marching into the sea, humans kill each other! How brutal!

QUAIL. Well, technically, you can shove that up your ass. (*Stalks off.*)

KATHI. (*To Chala.*) You seem cruel.

CHALA. Not to the animals, I'm not.

KATHI. Point of view, I guess.

CHALA. Now your Havasupai. Your Indians. They are a small tribe. They can fit into the ecology of this region.

KATHI. You wouldn't remove them?

CHALA. I don't think so. I want to see them. I *must* see them.

KATHI. Must? Why?

CHALA. We are proposing to take many more Indian tribes into national parks to protect them. In some places, like Venezuela, it's already done. The Yanomami people ...

KATHI. Let them go on hunting?

CHALA. Yes.

(*Commotion in the audience.*)

KATHI. Isn't that inconsistent with your—?

CHALA. No, no! They have lived in harmony with wild animals for centuries. They don't remove entire populations. They have to depend on them. Something your fishermen obviously never even thought about.

KATHI. Well, I guess there *is* a difference ...

STUBBS. (*Interrupting.*) Now he wants to take our fishing rods from us. Ask him how he would control animal populations if we *don't* hunt and fish.

CHALA. (*After translation, smiling.*) They never needed hunting *before* man came. It is not a matter of controlling animal populations. It never has been. It is a matter of controlling man. *He's* the overpopulated species. Control him! Not animals.

STUBBS. (*Rising and exiting left.*) Oh, bullshit!

CHALA. I only want to be fair. We've had a hundred years of killing wild animals. Now let us have a hundred years of not killing them.

KATHI. The animals would multiply.

CHALA. And starve. Nature controls them.

KASBOLT. I think he's *got* something, actually.

CHALA. Other religions around the world say that animal life is as sacred as human life. What's wrong with that? Your own Chief Seattle—you know of him? You know what he said? If we eliminate the animals, we will eliminate us.

JOE. (*Rising.*) Ted's motioning to load up. Your Eminence, we thank you.

They rose. Mozo Fernandez came up to Joe. "Well, he made it clear. I'll say that for him."

"Now you can see why it's such an odd idea to Americans, to Christians, and so on. To hundreds of millions of other people around the world it's general policy. He's asking, why not everybody?"

"But don't a lot of those people kill wild animals? How come?"

"Renegades," Joe replied. "Hunger. Medicine. Aphrodisiacs."

"You made Chala's point."

"So now you know."

"Thanks, Joe. Now we know."

Cynthia Kasbolt walked up, a frown on her face. "Why did Buck and Barry stay behind?"

"Cynthia, I think they're after the killer. I think they know who it is."

"Do you know who it is?"

"Yes. But the most important point is: I've got a very strong suspicion that there is one or more ahead, waiting to take a pot shot at Chala."

"Ahead? How could that be? Are you sure?"

"Pretty sure."

"How do you know?"

"I don't *know.* Just a suspicion."

"A very strong one?"

"Yeah."

"Joe, you're maddening."

"Thank you. I admire that in people."

Two hours later, as the sun fell behind cliffs, they landed and set up camp on a narrow shelf at the edge of the river.

The falling sun enriched the Redwall cliffs above Clear Creek and turned to somber purple as Buck and I waked from an afternoon of sleep.

Our quarry had turned up a left fork of the canyon. Less chance there to be discovered—in the very faint possibility (they must have thought) that someone would come looking for them. With water not far away, they could hide out for days, providing they brought enough food to last.

Buck and I had gone on to Clear Creek and found a cave in which Buck had camped before. We could sleep there by day, sheltered from the burning sun, and take our quarry tonight.

Now dusk had come. We sat at the mouth of the cave, the fading colors and soaring cliffs of the Redwall almost directly above. To the north, higher yet, we glimpsed the tree-covered ramparts of the North Rim—and the white layered walls of the Kaibab limestone.

"Up that canyon," Buck said softly, munching a biscuit, "is the highest waterfall in the Grand Canyon."

"I don't believe it," I said.

"I didn't think you would," Buck responded.

I listened for a moment. "I don't hear it. I don't see it. You're crazy."

"Well," Buck drawled as he dug into a can of roast beef, "it's not an ordinary waterfall. Indians call it *Cheyava*, meaning off and on."

I asked: "Sometimes flows, sometimes doesn't?"

"Well, I guess there's a seep and a trickle, at least, most of the year. But when snows melt on the North Rim, the waters seep down through all the layers of rock and come roaring out of a cave near the top of the Redwall. They cascade down eleven hundred feet over a series of ledges to the bottom of Clear Creek Canyon."

"Fantastic! Must be quite a sight."

"Yeah. You can find it from the South Rim if you know where to look. But after the spring runoff, there's not so much to see."

"Not many people see it, then?"

"Long hike over here. Or ride. I rode down last February..."

"February? You mean you guys don't hibernate in winter?"

Buck snarled: "Thank you for shutting up. I left the rim at zero degrees in three feet of snow, and by the time I got to the Tonto Platform here, I'd run out of snow and the temperature was sixty degrees. When I got to Cheyava the next morning, it was a mass of icicles for a thousand feet rows and rows of ice draped along ledges. All glistening and starting to melt in the afternoon sun."

"That's incredible. Next thing you're going to tell me is that we're not going to see it."

"Right."

"Buck, that's cruel and unusual punishment."

"We're not here on a sightseeing trip. Tell you what, if we get out of here alive——."

"What do you mean, if?"

"I'll take you to Havasupai. You were going to get there anyway until you aborted it."

"Buck, you're forgiven. Most beautiful place in the canyon, I'm told."

"Well, that's debatable, I suppose. But not for long."

I finished a can of peaches. "All right," I said, watching the gray shadows of dusk creep up the cliffs. "What about tonight?"

Buck hesitated a moment. "Well, about all we know is that they've got at least two horses..."

"I know," was my reply. "That makes sneaking up on them something of a problem...unless..."

"Unless we shoot first. Nothing doing. I want to take them alive."

"No, no, that's not what I was thinking. We'll take them alive, but we have to find a way to get to them."

"We can creep up only so far...."

"Granted. Then the horses give us away. That ought to work nicely."

Buck frowned. "That's what you *want?*"

"Do you have a Plan B?

Buck grinned. "Of course. And C. And D..."

"I'm listening."

"We could wait till they go to the creek for water."

"They may be on whiskey tonight."

"I mean for the horses. Or we wait till they take their horses out to graze."

I said nothing.

He asked: "You don't like B or C, do you?"

"No."

"Why not?"

"Buck, we don't have much time. Other people may be in danger. We've got to find out some things from these bastards and do it tonight."

"I copy. So you're going to stir up the horses and bring the guys out?"

"You make it sound easy. Of course! We don't know exactly where they are. It'll save time. I want them to come to *me.*"

Buck packed away his empty tins. "You're the one who's crazy. You got a pistol?"

"Nine millimeter Parabellum."

"That'll do. Let's get out of here. Follow me."

I put a restraining hand on his shoulder. "Not so fast..."

Buck looked at me with a scowl. "If you think you're going in there alone..."

"Buck, this is my fight, Chala's fight. It's not your fight. I don't want you to push into this any more than you have to."

Buck snorted. "This is park property."

"I know that."

"I'm responsible for law enforcement down here."

"I know that, too."

"This is *my* territory and *my* job."

"All of that doesn't mean anything right now. Buck, I'm going in there to get those guys and bring them out."

Buck sighed in mock despair. "You would deprive me of the glory?"

"You can have all the glory you want. You need brownie points, you can have 'em."

"I *don't* need brownie points, you bastard. I want those outlaws. They're on park property. They're mine."

"They killed a State Department official. They're mine."

"You work for the State Department?"

"No."

"Then they're mine. You think I'm going to let a tourist like you get into trouble while I stand back and twiddle my thumbs?"

I laughed. "Oh, you're not going to stand back and twiddle your thumbs. You're going to lead me to the trail, then

fade behind, and watch. Back me up. Come into it whenever you want. It may be *your* territory, but this is *my* job."

Buck looked me straight in the eye. "And if I refuse? I'm the ranking authority. I go first."

"And the Secretary of State talks to the Secretary of the Interior, who—as I recall the phrase—churns your ass to mush."

Buck stopped, his eyes narrowing to slits, a glum look of defeat and disgust on his face. He tried once more. "There's two of 'em out there. At least."

I grinned. "I've never had such favorable odds."

"You lie."

"Let's go."

Buck led the way out of the cave, down a steep slope, through a portal of rocks and back to the main trail.

We stopped to listen.

Somewhere in the distance a canyon wren sang its last glissando for the day. The western sky remained light, illuminating the cliffs but not the black shadows among fallen boulders.

We stepped carefully, unwilling to dislodge a rock and send it flying down a ravine. That would shatter the silence like machine-gun fire, echoing among the cliffs, reverberating a long distance in this pure, dry air. No doubt the men we sought had ears attuned to just such menacing sounds. The order of the night could not be denied: silence and stealth.

Seeing no one, hearing nothing, Buck turned to the left and edged slowly up the trail. He glanced backwards every minute or so to see that no one crept up on us while returning from the creek, say, with a canteen of water. I followed, eyes and ears alert.

My brain focused on the fact that a killer and an accomplice hid somewhere in the shadows beneath these walls.

After a few minutes, Buck paused and listened. Nothing. No wren. No footsteps. No voices. A distant cricket...nothing more.

Buck reached out and took my arm, bringing me up to a position in front. In the darkness, I saw him indicate a trail turning off and heading up a side canyon. A rough trail, for all I could see, uneven, piled with rocks, not even cleared of stunted mesquite.

I sneaked forward, eyes straining to detect loose rocks in the trail, to avoid kicking one, or turning an ankle on one and, worse yet, tripping and falling. No one could walk without making *some* sound, but I strove to move slowly, unevenly, so that our advance at least did not resemble human footsteps. Excruciatingly slow, I thought, but that's what it had to be in such quiet.

I paused a moment and looked behind. Buck had fallen back ten yards, barely visible now, obviously moving at the same uneven pace. I looked around, taking mental notes. Moving forward again, I tried to step on solidly placed rocks or little ledges—steps that involved no gravel or loosened rock. I moved my eyes constantly from wall to wall of this ravine, and from front to rear, but stayed mainly on the trail ahead. I hoped for a silhouette, a shadow, an amorphous gray form, or to hear someone *else's* footstep. Or perhaps, like last night, the indiscretion of a flashlight in the hands of one or both of the men we sought.

I listened intently for voices. The neigh of horses. The clank of a cup. Alas, we might be creeping up on figures sound asleep, who would wake with a start and come up in a blaze of flying lead...

Nothing yet. I crept on, oblivious to time, oblivious to anything but surprising and capturing the men who murdered—.

A sound... Or so I thought. In my state of red alert, even imaginary sounds seemed real and near and ominous. I stopped, stepped to the side of the trail, crouched, and listened.

Then I saw the light. Fire light! A very faint flickering against the wall of the canyon just ahead.

What luck! *You should have known,* my inner voice said. *Any dumb ox who would use a flashlight last night on the trail would no doubt light a fire tonight at camp. Regulations did not allow fires in this wilderness. An ordinary tourist would know that. Would use a tiny stove instead. Conduct himself so that no evidence remained of his passage...*

Not the Babbs. They could do no better, in their ignorance, than to lead the searchers directly to them. Why should they expect anyone near? In this silent wilderness, so far from human habitation?

A warning flashed in the back of my brain: suppose the light came from a tourist campfire. That would leave all our calculations awry. The culprits would have gotten away—somewhere else.

I dismissed the notion as soon as it came. A bona fide wilderness traveler would use a lantern for light, and not a campfire, not here in a desert so delicate and fragile.

Creeping closer, I listened for the warning of the horses...or the cocking of rifles. I drew out my pistol...

Another step. Pause. Another step. The horses must be tethered on the other side of camp.

Voices could now be heard. Drawing within twenty paces, I listened, but could not quite distinguish the words. I inched along. Rock to rock. Close enough, after a while, to begin to understand the conversation...

"...No, Blue, ya sonbitch! I meant the goddam horses. Don't ya think they gotta drink?"

"I'll take 'em down. First light o' day."

"You'll goddam take 'em down now. You know the way. They know the way."

"Oh, Smoke, I ain't in no shape to go down there. 'Sides, they might be somebody after us."

"Who?"

"The goddammed rangers, that's who."

"Oh, shit! You're skeered o' yer own fuckin' shadow."

Blue spat on the ground. "You're the one ought to be skeered. You're the one done the killin'..."

I peeped over the nearest fallen slab of sandstone. Two men sat hunkered around the little fire. Smoke Babb I recognized, from the encounter at the junction of the Little Colorado. Blue Babb I could scarcely see, the man's back being toward me. Blue seemed, however, to be cut of the same cloth—floppy hat, torn jeans, a stubble of beard visible when his head turned to the right.

I wasted no time, rising and saying in a calm, determined tone: "If one of you bastards makes a move, you get a slug right between the eyes."

The brothers jumped with a start, reaching for their rifles.

"FREEZE!" I shouted.

They froze in a state of shock, so surprised that they seemed unable to move, even by reflex action.

"Hands on your heads," I said, "unless you want 'em blown off."

Their hands went to their heads.

"Now stay right where you are and keep your eyes on the fire."

I saw their rifles stacked against a rock, barely visible at the edge of the circle of firelight. The Babbs said nothing, scarcely even moved.

"You are both about to be arrested for the murder of Hounto Chala," I lied.

Blue trembled and pointed toward Smoke. "He done it! He done it!"

Smoke shouted: "You goddammed sonbitch, I'll—"

I shouted: "Don't *move!* Keep those hands up!"

Moving away from the rock, I skirted the rim of firelight, picked up their rifles and laid them on the ground beside me.

Buck entered the firelight and sat on a rock opposite the Babbs. "You buzzards have just put yourselves away for a long, long time. They're gonna miss you in Kingman ..."

Blue blurted: "I swear! I ain't done nuthin'!"

Smoke: "I said *shut up,* you fuckin' sonbitch! Nobody can prove nuthin'!"

Buck said: "Where's Winnie? Where's Duke?"

Blue answered in a plaintive tone. "They went to Supai. They don't know Chala's dead already—."

I barked: "How do *you* know he's dead."

"You said so."

Smoke kicked Blue a resounding *whack!* on the side of the leg. "He don't know nuthin'. Now, shut up!"

"Ow-o-woo!" wailed Blue. "What the goddam hell d'ya do that fer?"

I advanced and stood above them. "We're gonna rope you up and take you back to Phantom tonight, then follow you up the trail to a van waiting to take you to the County Court House in Flagstaff."

"I didn't do it!" Blue yelled. "What ya want me fer?"

"We know you didn't do it, Blue. You don't need to worry. As an accessory to the crime, you ought to get off with good behavior in fifty years..."

Blue weakened. "Oh, Jee-suss!"

"Now, Smoke," I went on, lying, "you may not know it, but you killed a sovereign prince of a foreign nation..."

"You cain't *prove* that! You cain't prove nuthin'. I tol' ya that."

"...An officer of the United Nations, a guest of the United States, on federal property. Man, you may as well have killed a flock of FBI agents for all your ass is worth now. Do you know the penalty for all that?"

Blue shook his head back and forth. "Oh, Jee-suss'!" he wailed.

Smoke froze and kept silent.

"It's *hanging*," I said in authoritative tones. "This is the West, ain't it? Hangin'."

Blue bent over, unable to speak.

"*Sit up!*" I barked, "and get your hands back up where they belong."

Buck walked over to the men and withdrew pistols from their belts.

"I didn't do it!" Blue wailed.

I said: "We know that, Blue. We know a lot about what happened. Before and after. We know more than you could ever imagine. What we'd like to know, right here and now, is who paid you to do this."

Smoke barked in short syllables. "Who cares? Who cares? It's done! Ain't you glad? That black sonbitch was gonna take our guns away. A *nigger*. A *foreign nigger*. He was gonna make everbody stop shootin'. What'd ya expect? Ya oughtta be grateful to whoever killed him. He done it fer everbody. Done it to proteck our constitushnal right. Ain't you proud of him? You own a gun. You hunt. He did it to proteck everbody. Now git outta here and leave us alone."

"You didn't pay for this operation," I bounced back. "You guys ain't got enough money to buy a shit house. Who paid for this? Who paid you?"

Smoke: "Paid us? Fer what? Nobody paid us nuthin'."

"You're a liar. I don't want a goddamned runaround. If you want to save a little portion of your asses—or your necks—you had better come right down to the bottom line. Who paid you?"

Blue sniffled and shook his head. Smoke said nothing.

I gave them five minutes of silence in which to wilt, five minutes to consider...

At length, Buck said: "This is a waste of time, Barry. I don't think you need to pursue this any further."

I looked at him through slit eyes. "Why not?"

Buck waited a full minute before replying—to give the Babbs another chance to cave in. They said nothing.

"Because," said Buck, slowly, "I know who paid them."

I waited a few moments before replying. Then I said softly, as the little fire crackled. "So do I."

"We'd better move," said Buck. "We have to get word to Joe Muck and Lee Federico. As fast as we can."

Rusty Gorman, the wrangler, saddled up the horses and brought them to the hitching rack near Phantom Ranch dining room. Then he went around to the back, retrieved the body of the little Thai now neatly wrapped in canvas and brought it to the front. There he hoisted it on one of the horses, and tied it down for the trip to the rim.

A little boy, in cowboy hat and red bandanna, watched every movement.

"Whatcha got in the blanket, mister?"

Rusty Gorman's long experience with tourists had taught him never to let a question go unanswered. His standard response to "What is that flower?" remained simply: "Begonia."

"But they can't all be begonias," a tourist would say. To which he replied in classic candor: "Well, ma'am, it tries me like hell just to remember the names of these here mules, much less the names of all them flowers along the trail. So I calls 'em begonias. Most people don't know no difference no how."

The boy repeated the question. "What's in the blanket, mister?"

"Well," Rusty replied, "can you keep a secret?"

"Cross my heart!"

"Won't tell nobody? No matter what?"

"Hope to die!"

"Well, it's a dinosaur."

The little eyes widened. "Wow! A real one? A *live* one?"

"Live as they come."

"A *big* one?"

"Big as they come."

"A *mean* one?"

"Mean as they come."

"*How* mean?"

"Well, son, this one's so mean it comes out of there sometimes and bites off the heads of little boys who ask a lot of questions while I'm trying to saddle these hosses."

The boy turned and ran as fast as he could toward one of the cabins, shouting, "Mommy! Mommy!"

When the last of the ropes had been tied in place, Rusty called through the screen door into the dining room. "All ready, Mister Watkins."

Woody came out, day pack on his back, and inspected the horses.

"We'd better go up Bright Angel Trail. It's longer, but we'll come out at the village that way."

"Well, Mr. Watkins, the chief ranger's office is goin' to have a ambulance at the head of the Kaibab. They're goin' to take the body straight to Flagstaff."

"Flagstaff? Did they hear from the State Department what he wanted done in case of death?"

"Well, all they said was that they was goin' to cremate him and send the remains back to wherever he came from."

"Thailand."

"I guess so. Anyway, we're supposed to git on up the South Kaibab as soon as we can."

"Okay. You have the lunches?"

"Yes, sir."

"You got the sleeping bags packed from the raft luggage?"

"Yes, sir. Everything."

"Then let's go."

"Was they a ranger going up with us, Mister Watkins? Horse's all saddled."

"Yes."

The ranger came out the door and walked up to Rusty. Woody said: "You know each other?"

Rusty answered. "Sure do. How you this mornin', Miss Julie?"

At breakfast, little light came from the canyon dawn. Ted Quail gave the sixteen remaining passengers instructions.

"We will land at the mouth of Havasu Creek just after sunup. That's where you leave the river and leave us. It's a tough hike up to the village, nearly ten miles. That's why we're getting an early start, so you'll have some shade part of the way. The trail crosses Havasu Creek at least half a dozen times on the way, and you'll be up to your armpits in water at times. So put everything in your day pack so you can hold it over your heads."

"What about the rifles?" asked Dalton Stubbs.

"Rifles. Everything. You'll have to keep them out of the water. You'll also go through a narrow passage up through the tunnel at Mooney Falls. It's tight and its tricky, so don't take much stuff with you."

"What about our sleeping bags?"

"You'll be guests of the Supais so you won't need them. We'll take your sleeping bags, and anything else you don't

want to take with you, down to Lake Mead, then around to Hualapai Hilltop. That's where we'll meet you in four days. Anything else?"

No answer.

"Then load up."

The run to the Havasu Creek landing did not take long. As the first raft headed for shore, Joe said to Ted: "Good God! Where we gonna land?"

He counted twenty-three assorted rafts, canoes and dories tied to the rocky cliff in a complex of lines and lashings.

Ted eased the raft against one of those already moored, and tied his line to theirs. Rudy Vogel and Jerry Elliott moored their rafts to the lines of still others. When the three vessels had been secured, the passengers crawled over rafts to reach the rocky ledges and step out on a ledge. Joe looked back.

Most of the float vessels glowed with luminescent orange or yellow. One stood out in a dirty pink.

"Oh, oh!" Joe said to Cynthia. "The Goons are here. *Now* I'm sure."

"I guess so," Cynthia said, then frowned. "Woody ordered those guys out of the canyon at Phantom and their raft confiscated. Didn't anyone follow up on that?"

Joe scowled. "We got diverted."

B. J.: "If we find them up Havasu Canyon, we'll immobilize them."

Joe wanted to ask how B. J. meant that, but he thought he knew. Handcuffs, for example. Blindfolds... Bullets...

The climb up rocky ledges above the Colorado River involved tricky footing and jumps across crevices, but soon they stood on a small ridge and looked up Havasu Creek.

The red rock canyon before them, narrow by standards to which they had become accustomed, appeared to be a rich oasis in the desert. The canyon floor, covered with trees, shrubs and arbors of grape vines, exhibited a rich green in contrast to the dry rock walls around. The crystal waters of Havasu Creek poured into one emerald pool after another. The water's passage had been diverted unknown years ago by massive sandstone blocks fallen from the cliffs or transported downstream in times of flood. The sound of falling water echoed from the cliffs. The spectators saw no sign of a trail, except a ledge on the right, just wide enough to allow a fully laden backpacker to pass, and a rocky shore across the creek, where one could climb up to some hidden trail.

In the distance—well, this curving canyon had no distance. Steep slopes, hidden in shadow, cut off the view beyond three hundred yards.

"Nothing in the Garden of Eden could match this," Joe said.

Angel added: "If there were a Shangri-La, this is it."

Kent Thomas: "It does seem like an oasis, doesn't it?"

Neff Neilson came by. "The creek issues from the sand a short way above the village. It is the life blood of the Supais."

Kent said: "I can believe that. But this creek must also be vulnerable to flash floods?"

"It can kill," Neff agreed. "Flood once took out the village. Mighty violent sometimes. Very dangerous to hikers who don't stay alert."

Cynthia came up and said: "The water's so *clear*. The deep pools are so *green*."

"They're full of calcium carbonate, though," Neff said. "This water has flowed underground for long distances, largely through the Redwall limestone. That gives the water a real charge—hard water you'd call it. Then where it splashes, dries and evaporates regularly, it leaves a deposit. That builds up drapes and terraces that we call travertine. Calcium carbonate also precipitates to form little dams. That's why you have hundreds of pools all up the canyon."

Cynthia asked: "Can we swim?"

"That's up to Joe," Neff answered.

"Of course," Joe answered. "But keep your rifles dry."

He saw the assistant chief ranger and called him over. "B. J., will you try to keep everyone together today?"

"Yes, sir. I'll bring up the rear. Keep moving 'em along."

"Everybody should remain alert that there's some guns up there, waiting for us. Did you give Chala a park service hat?"

"We did. He's still down at the rafts, saying goodbye to all the crew."

Cynthia asked: "What about the cowboy hat?"

Joe answered: "Thanks for reminding me."

He untied it from the back of his pack and looked at it.

"It's not the same hat it was," he lamented. "Torn. Crushed. Bullet hole through it."

"It belongs to Chala," she said. "You gave it to him."

"Aw, he wouldn't want it now. Maybe I should take it back."

Kent Thomas: "What kind of protocol is that? You'll provoke an international incident."

"I'll send him another one. I've got six more at home."

Kent smiled. "I know him. He'll mount it on his wall."

Cynthia: "So what are you going to do with this one?"

Joe answered matter-of-factly. "Wear it."

Gasps came from those around him.

Cynthia: "Are you crazy?"

"Yes."

Dee Dunn: "You want to get shot at?"

"Yes."

Kent Thomas: "Joe, you're mad. We've already had one fatality under that hat. It's enough."

Cynthia: "Please spare us. Put it away. Better yet, *throw* it away. You'll make us all nervous."

Joe held up his hand. "I am deeply touched by all this concern. But to tell you the truth, this hat has a very important use yet. I would very much like them to shoot at me."

Kent: "Why, for God's sake?"

"One good way of getting them to reveal their position."

Cynthia spread her hands. "At the cost of your own life? Isn't that silly? B.J., can't you stop him?"

Joe said: "Cynthia, I haven't the slightest intention of dying..."

"Most people don't," she said. "What are you trying to say?"

"Well, to be very practical about it, I'd rather they shoot at me than at Chala."

Kent said: "Very noble, Joe. But that seems to be taking bravery a step too far. Can't you manage something so that *neither* of you will be shot at?"

Joe, smiling: "I have. An ingenious plan. A masterpiece of strategy."

He walked over to a pile of shrubbery and retrieved a stick about four feet long. Pulling out a pocket knife he cut a notch about two inches from one end.

Kathi LeClair came to the group and asked: "What's going on?"

Cynthia replied: "Joe's on a suicide mission."

"Good," Kathi said. "That'll make a great story. What's the deal?"

Cynthia: "He's going to wear that cowboy hat."

Kathi: "What for? Is he crazy? He'll get shot."

"Of course, he will. He *wants* to get shot."

"Splendid," said Kathi. "That'll make an even better story. American sacrifices self for African prince. Twist of history."

"Oh, Kathi. How can you jest at a time like this? He mustn't do it!"

"Why not?" Angel asked. "History is full of such daring feats. He might just pull this off whatever it is."

Joe said: "Watch."

He tied the stick to thongs attached to the shoulder straps of his backpack, then hoisted the pack onto his shoulders. When this had been done, the stick protruded about thirty-six

inches above his right shoulder. Then he handed Cynthia the cowboy hat and a piece of leather boot thong. Backing off a step, he bent over, bringing the end of the stick close to her.

"Now," he said, "tie the hat to the notch I cut."

"Joe! I won't do it! I won't aid and abet this ridiculous—."

Joe: "I thought a good ranger always wanted to try out new ideas..."

"As long as they are government ideas," she replied.

The circle erupted in laughter as Cynthia tied the hat to the stick. When Joe stood, the hat soared above his head.

B. J., standing on the sidelines, said: "Joe, you're ten feet tall now. I think I see what you're up to. You think it's going to work?"

Joe laughed. "No."

"Well, it *could.*"

"Sure it could. I wouldn't try this trick on a sophisticated killer. It's too silly. No intelligent person would be taken in by it. But with the Goons, it might just work."

"Okay," B. J. said. "Let's go find out."

Joe took up his carbine. The rest grabbed their rifles.

They descended along the rocky ledge to Havasu Creek, waded into the water, crossed over and headed up the trail on the other side.

Kathi LeClair saw Ted Quail sitting sullen and morose beside the trail, watching the others depart. She decided not to follow them up the trail just yet.

"B.J.," she said, "if you don't mind I'd like to talk to Ted. May I catch up with you in a few minutes?"

B.J. nodded assent and went on up the trail.

Kathi turned to Ted. "You don't look very happy."

"Well, Jesus Christ," he said, voice glum and, for a change, subdued, glad to have the chip knocked off his shoulder, "how would you feel if they took away freedom of the press?"

She didn't answer for a few moments, not quite sure what he meant by that statement. He had not looked at her when he spoke. His eyes, averted, seemed glazed, fixed on the rippling green waters of the creek.

"Why do you say that?" she asked.

"Sometimes I feel hemmed in," he answered. "Like it's not my country any more. People are telling me I can't smoke.

If I get married, people will tell my wife she can't have an abortion. I get the feeling that every American is trying to pry into my business, my freedom, my whole life. They already tell me I can't hunt or fish at certain times of the year... Why don't people just mind their own God-damned business?"

He trailed off and became silent.

Kathi said: "Well, Ted, they also tell us we can't murder. We live in a society. We're a colonial species."

"Like pelicans."

"Sure. If a pelican does something against the colony, he's edged out."

"So we've become pelicans. That's what I mean. Robots. Zombies. Wooden soldiers. We may as well have wooden guns. Don't you see how dangerous this guy Chala is to what America stands for?"

"I understand what you're saying, Ted. I wasn't quite thinking of it that way. You're true to yourself—because there's still something of the frontiersman in you. The trapper, the miner, the explorer. They depended on their guns. Wildlife was plentiful. But Americans are also very humane, Ted. And a lot of them are just plain weary of guns. Americans *started* the national park idea so they could *keep* animals from being hunted..."

Ted spoke softly. "I don't argue with that. I think that's good."

"And they learned from the passenger pigeon experience that you just can't keep shooting wild animals, or else one day you wake up and find they're all gone."

"That's obvious."

"There have come to be too many hunters."

Ted grumbled. "That's obvious, too. That's part of what I don't like."

"It's not the same wilderness it was..."

He shook his head in disgust. "I feel like going to Alaska."

"You want to move on, like the trapper, until some day there won't be anywhere else to go."

He looked at her for the first time. "You think my breed is dying?"

It was a surprise question, but in a way she almost anticipated it. "I don't know. I haven't gone into this. I wish I could. I wish I were a pro. Chala's a pro. A biologist. He takes the animals' side. I suppose someone—some American—could say that he wished to God there'd been a Chala back when the passenger pigeons were disappearing..."

"I know that. I know that. I hear you. But I feel defensive. Am I being pushed back into a corner? If so, I'm gonna come out fighting. Am I?"

"Ted, I think you are."

"Why? Why do you say that? You're a journalist. You talk to a lot of people..."

"Well, I don't specialize. I try to stay neutral. I'm trying to stay neutral in this Chala business. It certainly has two sides. But I begin to sense that more and more people are taking the side of the animals. We get reports on the wires—we can't publish them all. There's a whole division of the United Nations devoted to the environment. That wasn't there before. We have the Environmental Protection Administration. That wasn't there before. Ted, I get the feeling you *are* being crowded."

"Crowded out? Is that what you mean?"

"Well, at least being pushed. You're losing your constituency."

Ted's head snapped around. "What do you mean by that?"

"We know that a lot of people love *wild* animals. We get millions of visitors to these parks. They'll vote for the animals if they perceive a threat. Any threat. The animals have a voting constituency. And people in Congress are discovering this."

"So?"

"I interviewed a professor of range management last month. He said: 'If I say we need this or that valley for sheep grazing, and the local Audubon Society says we need it for

bird protection habitat, I've lost the game. By next year it'll be a bird reserve. Sheep don't have near the constituency that wild birds have.'"

Ted dropped his head in gloom. She felt suddenly that she looked at an endangered species, a lonely hunter, ready to go beyond the next mountain range, looking for the next frontier...

She said nothing more for a while. He had become sullen and morose again. She thought she knew now how he felt. There could be no use in discussing the Chala proposal with him. It had become a dagger in his heart. He had become a buffalo hunter with no more buffalo to hunt. The hunters of passenger pigeons had themselves become a dying species...

She wanted to say that to him, but she could not bring herself to do it. He now seemed to her a sadder figure than ever. She could think of nothing to cheer him up. He had already spoken of the hunter as a dying species. He would fight. He would defend himself. The minutes passed...

Then she said: "Ted, you must not think of yourself as a dying species. There will always be hunting reserves of *some* kind. Some place where the animals will replenish themselves. We have lots of wildlife reserves where hunting is allowed..."

He looked at her with unexpectedly gentle eyes. Then he looked back at the creek again. "Thank you, Kathi," he said, softly. "I suppose I needed that. And I guess I can't be too tough on Chala..."

She dared to ask why not.

"Because," he answered slowly and carefully, his eyes still far away, "I like tigers as much as he does."

Kathi responded with dignity. "Ted, I appreciate that."

He raised his eyes to the cliffs above for a moment, then let his gaze fall to the creek. When he spoke, the words came in subdued tones.

"The meek are inheriting the earth and there isn't a God-damned thing I can do about it."

He fell silent and Kathi knew the conversation had come to an end. She wanted to say that if Chala represented the meek, then he's got problems, too. He's the one the assassins are after. But one look at Ted's face told her not to reopen the interview.

She rose and started up the trail.

They made their way up the trail, rifles slung over their shoulders, eyes on the rims above, the shady grapevine thickets along the creek, and the trunks of cottonwood trees beside the trail.

In such a paradise, Joe's mind became mesmerized. He ducked his high-flying hat so that he could pass beneath low-hanging limbs. He turned sideways to avoid an overhang of red sandstone.

The hours advanced as though in a dream. The sunlight filtered through leaves and fell on the trail like empty images of coins. Water dashed into pools, calmed, and roared out again. Cool copses of seepwillow and bowers of grape tempted them to stop and rest.

They went on as the heat rose. Sunlight poured into the canyon and the shimmering heat had nowhere to go. Joe felt perspiration oozing down his neck, his back, his shoulders. His eyes, protected by sunglasses, grew tired from the constant searching of shadows, cliffs, ravines and rims for ominous human movements. Sometimes the procession paused in the shade beneath a cliff, where the hikers cooled their dripping brows.

Chala also wandered as though in a dream, surrounded by such green after miles and miles of red rock on the river. His bodyguards preceded him. Neff and Angel walked behind, along with Kathi, who took on some of the little Thai's duties as translator.

For a long time, Chala queried Angel: Is this reservation within the park? For all practical purposes, yes, but technically, no. Did the Supai Indians have rights as citizens? Could the Indians vote? Could they carry on a business? Were they free?

Yes... Yes... Yes...she kept saying. This is their country. This is their home. This is their America.

But aren't we in a national park?

Not exactly.

Doesn't a human village here violate your rules?

The Indians were here before the park was.

Chala erupted in glee. "Exactement! Exactement!" You give these rights to your native peoples. Why not to native animals?

Animals do have rights in national parks.

Back to the Indians. Do you allow them to remain primitive?

That's a strange question.

No it isn't. Why do you say strange?

Well, we don't regard them as primitive.

You educate them?

They educate themselves. Many go to college.

Ah, but certainly you don't let them have television. It would corrupt them. Destroy their original culture.

They can have whatever they want. Besides, there is a lot of education on television today.

But are you sure you want to bring them into the future?

The future? They're *in* the future. What does that have to do with it?

Would you allow them to modernize themselves?

It's not for us to say. They govern themselves. They have a tribal council. That's up to them. Do you understand?

Would they *want* to modernize themselves?

You'll have to ask them that. How can anyone dictate *that* to them? Sometimes there are factions in tribes, some wanting to preserve the old ways, some wanting to adopt new ways. It's not always easy.

Mademoiselle, you have given me new perspective. You Americans are experts. You don't know how many times we have faced these problems with primitive tribes...really primitive. Governments wondering what to do with them, how to treat them... Leave them alone.

They could have gone on for hours. Between the questions and the uphill climb, Chala had to stop for breath. In nearly every shady spot he paused to take in his surroundings and marvel at the narrow canyon, the deep blue sky... and the miracle of Indians with freedom.

And so the day went. They talked. They swam. They climbed past Beaver Falls, a roaring cascade on the creek. They met other hikers on the trail and stopped to chat. Chala remained a celebrity, as before, and Joe had a difficult time pulling him away.

They stopped for lunch and a refreshing swim in the pools on terraces downstream from Mooney Falls, 110 feet high. The water cascaded with a sound like thunder into a partially sunlit amphitheater. Neff showed them wild celery and orchids growing at the edges of pools.

After lunch they climbed through tortuous tunnels in the travertine surrounding Mooney Falls. Joe had to take off his hat and stick in order to negotiate those passages. Chala had a close fit, but went through laughing.

Hiking on, they came to Havasu Falls. Standing on a rise they looked down at "one of the most peaceful vales on earth," Neff called it. Chala agreed. To the right, Havasu

Falls poured with a mighty roar down 85 feet into rippling pools of turquoise waters. Travertine dams held the waters, which overflowed into pool after pool, terrace after terrace, on their way downstream.

Beyond rose soft and cooling green thickets, and beyond that a sandy-floored side canyon in the Redwall limestone.

"Carbonate Canyon," said Angel. "Miners worked up there for a while. You can still see the mine shafts and tailings slopes. But there wasn't enough lead or zinc to make it worthwhile. Nothing much came of it."

Chala stood transfixed. The rangers remained on alert—swimmers in the creek, hikers on the trail, campers downstream. Joe tried to move the party onward and upward, if slowly. He wanted to allow Chala and his aides as much time as possible to view the scene—but he considered security precautions paramount.

Anyway, he congratulated himself on good going so far. The pink raft told him the Goons hid out up here somewhere. He had no doubt they would soon be heard from. Would they wait until arrival at Supai? Would they have horses to make their escape? Would they somehow steal up and strike at night? Then race away in the darkness?

Once more, Joe felt that empty feeling of being unprepared and at a disadvantage. Like going under the bridge again. A killer could escape. They could not pursue. The Goons were stupid, but they could do their job, maybe with some accidental good luck. No doubt they hoped that the hunting world would idolize them. Joe had no way to—.

A shot exploded, echoing from wall to wall in this idyllic vale, fading rapidly under the roar of the waterfall. Joe felt something tear through his elevated cowboy hat and impact in the earthen slope above the trail...

Julie, Woody and Rusty neared the south rim as their horses labored up the trail in the increasing heat of midday. They arrived at the Fern Quarry, a site where fossil ferns had been discovered in the Hermit shale.

"Why not lunch here?" Woody suggested, dismounting.

Rusty opened the saddlebags and took out three box lunches.

"Tell me," Woody said to Rusty as they sat to eat, "have you heard of my proposal to put tramways down into the canyon?"

"Yes, sir."

"What do you think of it?"

"Well, sir, if you please, I don't much like it."

"Don't like it? Why not? It would sure save you a lot of sweat and dust."

"Well, Mister Watkins, I never thought there was anything wrong with sweat and dust."

"But all the heat. The hard work."

"That's my job."

Woody's jaw fell. "You *like* it?"

"Yes, I guess I do. A little dust ain't gonna kill no one. Not in my view anyway. Tourists eat a lot of it down here and come up smilin'."

Julie couldn't help but break into a smile, but she said nothing.

Woody went on. "But tramways would be a lot better for tourists, wouldn't they? Easier. Safer. Quieter."

"Well, sir, I may be wrong, but I don't think tourists want it that way. I think they ought to come down like this. On the trail. Get more out of the canyon itself."

"Some can't, Rusty. Too old. Too weak. Too fat. And what about the disabled?"

"Well, sir, I just don't think we *ought* to make it easy to get down here."

"You'd deprive people of getting into the canyon?"

"No. They can walk in or ride a mule."

"What about old people? Why not give them a chance?"

"Well, sir, they've *had* their chance."

Woody's eyes flew wide open at that. "What? That's a cruel thing to say, Rusty."

The cowboy looked out across the vast expanse of canyon. "I think we ought to leave this whole canyon for the young. Well, of course, I mean the young at heart, too. Lots of old people hike down here. I say save the canyon for them that wants to walk down into it. Let 'em explore, hike, git t'know the wilderness. They ain't no other experience like this, Mister Watkins. I'd like people to be proud o' themselves for hikin' down here. Havin' the gumption to do it."

Woody guffawed. "That's old fashioned, Rusty. You have to bring yourself up to date."

"Well, sir, if it means tramways, then I guess I belong in some other time."

"Oh, Rusty, I have a wonderful plan. I'm going to put in a tramway at Hermit's Rest, another one down Bright

Angel Canyon, another one at Grandview Point down to Horseshoe Mesa. Then Desert View. And one for the North Rim. Think of it!"

"I am, Mr. Watkins. Way it is now, most people are pretty satisfied just to come to the rim and look down. That's enough."

Woody snarled. "Well, it's not enough for me!"

At this point, Julie spoke for the first time. She had listened to the conversation with her eyes averted, looking either at the ground, or far off down the west end of the gorge—which now simmered in the heat of midday. "Well, Rusty," she said. "I don't think you need to worry. As Inner Canyon Ranger, I've been asked to testify on that proposal at a Congressional hearing in Washington this October."

Rusty's eyes turned to her with a kind of simple, hopeful look. "Would you now, Miss Julie? Well, what would you say?"

"Same things you just said, Rusty. I'd oppose it."

She looked at Woody, but saw no reaction. His eyes dropped from Rusty to the ground, narrowing. His brow furrowed slightly.

"I'd oppose it," Julie went on, "because it would do immeasurable damage. Ruin the wilderness aspect. Sully the whole idea of a national park. By the time I get to Washington, I'll have a hundred other reasons. I'm interviewing hikers. Mule riders. They're all against the idea. One hundred per cent."

Rusty smiled and looked away, immensely satisfied with himself.

Woody's face became a showcase of hidden fury, but he said nothing. The three of them sat for a few moments, looking at the ground, avoiding each other's eyes.

Rusty broke the silence. He pointed to one of the horses. "I don't like the way May Belle's standing. I'm going to have to work on her shoes. If I don't, you won't be able to ride her on up to the top, Miss Julie."

"No problem, Rusty," she responded. "It's not far to the rim from here. I think I'd like to walk out anyway."

She rose. Woody said: "That's a good idea. I think I'll walk, too."

Rusty went over to the mare and began to examine its hoof. Woody and Julie started up the trail into the Coconino switchbacks.

Julie took the lead, but Woody remained close behind.

"Julie," he said, "I think it might be wise for you to reconsider your position. On this tramway proposal of mine, that is."

"Yes, sir?" she said, blankly.

"Because you're an employee of this park. We're talking park policy. And if you're against it, then you might have some problems."

She looked neither to right nor left. "Problems?"

"Yes. We have to be a team, you know. There's no room for private thinking in government."

"What kinds of problems?"

"Well, you might not be invited back as inner canyon ranger next summer, if you're against park policy."

She responded slowly. "Is this park policy? Or is it Watkins policy?"

"Well, it really doesn't matter to you, does it? I approve all applications for service employment in this park. If you want your job back..."

Julie frowned. "What you're really saying is that you want me to shut up about it?"

"I guess that would be the general idea."

"Not go to Washington? Not testify on it?"

"I guess not. No."

"If I do, I'll lose my job?"

"Well, that part is just between the two of us, Julie. A kind of friendly warning, you might say, from me to you."

"A word to the wise?"

"Yes, That's it."

"Sounds more like a little friendly blackmail to me."

"Ah, Julie, really... We like your work here. We'd like to see you back."

"Should I ask for a hundred-dollar kicker? Or is this just a matter of holding my job hostage? What are you getting into next?"

They zigged and zagged their way up the switchbacks. The bright tan rocks of the Coconino glared in the sun. They adjusted their sunglasses. Neither could see the other's eyes.

"Why are you so heated up on this subject, Woody?" she asked. "The tramways, I mean. You know full well it doesn't stand a chance. The park has more important problems than that. Like air pollution."

The tone of his voice shifted. She could tell that he was getting madder. "Come on, Julie. There are millions of people who would go to the bottom of this canyon if those tramways were just *there.* You know that full well."

"Well, Woody, that's not really the point, is it? People can drive to the bottom of Zion Canyon if that's the kind of experience they want."

He snarled: "They want to go to the bottom of *this* canyon. They're not at Zion. Or anywhere else. They're *here.* There isn't any other Grand Canyon."

"That's my whole point. That was Rusty's point. We're supposed to leave it alone *because* it's the Grand Canyon. My God, it's the most beautiful gorge on earth. We're supposed to take care of it. Not screw it up with tramways. People don't want to see all those superstructures going down the Supai, the Redwall..."

"I can hide them. You won't even see them."

"Woody, that sounds like an argument at the point of desperation."

"Well, I have to be frank with you, Julie. When you have the chairman of the appropriations committee asking for something, you don't turn him down. You ought to be bureaucrat enough to know that."

Julie stopped and turned toward him. "Senator Sweeney?"

"Yes."

"Senator Sweeney doesn't run this park. Or any park."

"Of course. But he and his committee give or withhold money for everything the parks do. There isn't an administrator alive who would thwart the Senator's wishes."

"Didn't Senator Sweeney appoint you to this job?"

"No. The Secretary of the Interior did."

Julie persisted. "Without prior experience. He did it at the request of Senator Sweeney. I remember now. It was in the papers, even back in Lexington. They all said you weren't qualified, but you got the job anyway. How'd you manage that?"

"Julie, Senator Sweeney happens to be a very good friend of mine. Of my family."

"*Aha!*" she said. "I'm beginning to see the light, now. He has a lot of big national parks in his state that he wants to open up to hunting. So he really sent you here to embarrass the people running the parks. Needle them. Harass the personnel. Get them off base. Bring up old ideas that have already been consigned to the garbage can."

"Julie, that's probably about it. Who's going to oppose Senator Sweeney? That's *power*, Julie." He brandished a fist.

"*Real power!* You get on his side and you can have whatever you want."

She looked at him squarely. "You finish here, you go to something bigger?"

"That's the way of the government, Julie. Rank has its privileges. You ought to learn that some time."

"I'm learning a lot," she replied. "And I don't like it."

She turned and went on up the trail.

Woody followed. "He could get me appointed Lieutenant Governor, Julie. And from there I could run for governor, and then for Congress. Maybe even the Presidency. The park people know that. They don't give me any flak. We get along fine. I don't have to worry about them."

"That's good."

"But I do worry about you, Julie. You're anti-government. You're against progress. You're not park service. You don't know when to follow the line..."

She whirled in the trail. "*You're* the one who's not park service! You're just trying to run up a lot of victories at the parks' expense. No matter what the merits. You think you can ride over anybody and get whatever you want as long as you've got hold of Senator Sweeney's coattails... Violate regulations. Blackmail people... But a lot of us don't knuckle under. We inform the public of what's going on. Then they write Congress. We scare you, don't we? Scare the hell out of you!"

She whirled around without waiting for an answer and started up the trail again. Hidden by sunglasses, her eyes flashed with anger. Some backpackers approached, going down the trail. Julie hailed them warmly. Then her thoughts swirled furiously in her head again.

They had nearly reached the top of the Coconino sandstone when she turned again and confronted him.

"And now it begins to dawn on me. I should have seen through it before. Senator Sweeney's state is also a *fur-trade* state. Isn't it, Woody? Senator Sweeney doesn't want all those

jobs threatened by silly ideas like giving wild animals legal rights. By things like Chala's proposal."

"Poff, Julie, I doubt if he ever even *heard* of Chala."

"Don't feed me that, Woody. He must have called you and given some instructions about the Chala project. Or else you heard of it first, and you called *him*. Offering to nip in the bud an idea that would, as you put it, endanger his entire state. Then, of course, he wanted *you* to get rid of Chala! Wouldn't that be a boon to the fur trade? To all hunters? He gave you instructions about Chala. Set you up as point man. After all, you were his spy anyway. How could you refuse? Another feather in your cap, right? Your ambitions would soar. If Sweeney wants to expand hunting in the national parks of his state, then you would be just the man to handle Chala. It all comes together, Woody."

He scowled. "You couldn't even begin to prove a silly story like that."

"Oh, couldn't I? You told us at Redwall Cavern that you didn't hunt. That very night you talked about your hunting rifle. That brands you as a liar."

"Julie, I think at this point I'd better give you a powerful warning about making accusations like that. You're out of your territory."

"Am I, Woody? I'm inner canyon ranger, if you'll recall. Law enforcement in the canyon, remember? Then when we met the Babb Brothers at the Little Colorado Junction, guess who informed them that Chala was the one wearing a cowboy hat?"

"Julie... I warn you..."

"Then you said their raft would be confiscated at Phantom and they would be required to walk out of the canyon. Remember that? You didn't follow up on it, Woody. Gave no orders. I was watching you. I was waiting. I was going to ask, but I held back. You didn't *want* them to leave. Why not? You knew one would try to kill Chala at the bridge, because you planned it that way. And if that didn't work, you instructed the other Babbs to go on down the river.

You ordered them to try again... How did they know the party was going to Supai? You are the one who drew up the whole plan..."

"Julie..."

"Barry and Buck got on to you the same way. I see it all, now. Only they tabbed you before I did. They went to Clear Creek."

Woody went rigid. "What?"

"They went to Clear Creek. You know what they found over there, don't you? I don't. But you do. Because you planned it. And now Barry and Buck know. What *did* they find, Woody? Does it worry you?"

Woody clenched and reclenched his fists. He stood first on one foot, then the other. He looked at the ground, then off the edge of the trail down into the canyon.

Heat waves had begun to melt the sharp lines of the inner buttes and ridges. Perspiration dripped down his neck...

Julie continued, her mind working faster. "You paid the Babb Brothers to do your dirty work for you. How many thousands did the fur people send you to fund all this? You ought to be good at budgets. How many? Twenty thousand? Thirty? We can check your bank deposits. You're trapped, Woody..."

A clatter of hooves on the trail reached their ears as a string of pack mules bore down on them from the switchbacks above. Julie and Woody moved to the outer edge of the trail, in accordance with custom, to let the mules pass. The wrangler hailed them with a wave and went past.

As they balanced at the edge of the trail, Woody watched the mules going by, the huge packs on their backs, almost touching and grazing his elbow.

He looked at Julie, teetering at the edge, watching the mules going on down the trail.

Suddenly, he grasped both hands and swung out against Julie's shoulder, hitting her with a resounding wallop, and knocking her off the trail, out into the open air.

At the first sound of the shot, muffled though it had been by the roar of Havasu Falls, the hikers fell to the trail and stayed there. Since the bullet impacted the wall high above the trail, Joe deduced from its trajectory that it had come from the vale below.

He pulled the stick from his pack and tossed it and the hat on the trail. Calling the rangers, he issued instructions.

"Dalton, would you watch below for any movement? And especially for more than one person. Don't fire at anyone. Don't *anybody* fire at anyone. Could be tourists and campers down there. Cynthia, I'd appreciate it if you could coordinate with Dalton and keep track of any second or third person you see with suspicious movements. That includes under the waterfall. Everywhere. If anyone tries to escape from down there, apprehend him. Disable him. But don't kill him."

She nodded. Joe went on: "Mozo, could you go back down the trail and keep hikers away from here? People may want to gather and gawk. Keep 'em away."

"Roger."

"Eddie, if you could do the same up the trail. Keep hikers away. Also, I think it would be wise to find cover up there for Chala, and, if you're sure it's safe, take him and his party there. Get them behind some rocks or something. Out of sight. Neff, you and Angel go with them, help Eddie find better cover than this."

They acknowledged and began to creep up the trail with Chala, the bodyguards, Sam, Dee, Kathi, Dietrich and Kent.

Joe motioned B. J. to accompany him. "Let's go down and git 'em."

Bending low, they slipped back down the trail. Under cover of shrubbery, they stepped off the trail and worked their way down into the streamside forest.

They moved very slowly. Joe felt relieved that they didn't have to worry about making sounds that might give them away. The pervasive roar of the waterfall, amplified by the travertine and limestone amphitheater into which the water plunged, filtered everywhere. But they traded this for the disadvantage of not being able to hear any sound that might give away the location of their quarry.

Joe stopped and scanned the shadows, placid dark waters of the creek, clumps of grass, shrubbery, and tree trunks.

They slipped into a long, dark pool, holding aloft their packs and rifles. Sinking to their armpits, they waded across, grasped a small tree trunk and rose carefully out on the other side. Putting their packs back on, they started upstream through a patch of tall grass.

Joe moved by inches, as I had taught him to do. This took extraordinary measures of patience. It irked him to have to go slowly, when crashing through the forest might flush the enemy. But hikers and swimmers could be around, including children, and somebody could get shot that way. So he held back, pausing repeatedly to look for anything out of place—a rifle barrel, perhaps. The toe of a boot. An odd shape or

shadow behind a tree. Something to see before being seen, according to Joe's Law of Pursuit.

B.J. worked the scene as well, visually scouring a range of 360 degrees. It took time and patience, despite how tense they had become. So many things to scan! Thousands of leaves, twigs, limbs. Blade after blade of tall grass. Even sudden movements that startled them like the flitting of a bridled titmouse from limb to limb at the base of the shrubbery. And what about a rattlesnake, come to drink? Just the kind of cool, shady place, Joe calculated, that any self-respecting rattler would seek on a summer day.

The sun dropped behind a cliff to the west. Sunset had come—in mid-afternoon.

That darkened the shadows. Bad news, Joe said to himself. Now it will be even harder to see anything.

Through an opening in the trees, he glimpsed a fallen cottonwood trunk and peered carefully all around it for any telltale hat, rifle barrel, or shadow out of place. Then the standing trunk of a dead cottonwood. Same scrutiny.

Same result. Nothing.

He looked back up at the huddled figures on the trail. Most had continued upward very slowly, keeping low. He could barely see them. Eddie Roff must have scouted a hiding place above them, out of sight of the creek.

Another step. Another scan. Rifles at the ready.

Suddenly, B. J. touched Joe's arm...motioning that he wanted to take the lead. Joe looked quickly ahead, saw nothing, whispered: "But—."

Putting his finger to his lips, B. J cautioned silence and stepped ahead.

Gazing intently at the upper end of the shadowy pool, B. J. tensed. His eyes did a quick dance toward Joe, then back again. He had come upon something, Joe deduced from that fleeting look. Unmistakable eyebrow language which said: "I can see it but you can't. And I haven't time now to go over it with you. Stay just behind me."

Joe followed B. J. as the ranger slipped forward like a black panther through the grass. Joe became intensely curious, expectant. Following closely, he frowned, wondering what the ranger had seen that he hadn't. Wondering what all this caution meant.

B. J. stopped and pointed. Joe followed the direction of the arm into a mass of grass, tree stems and dark water. Something must be mightily camouflaged, Joe thought, if B. J. could see it and he could not. Not even with squinting. He could not see a thing out of the ordinary.

That had happened to Joe before, in the thick tropical forests of the Amazon basin, where something would fly up into the tall shadowy trees—never to be seen again.

Frustrating! To B. J., something so easily seen. To Joe, nothing visible whatever. If a killer lay there, surely the bulk of the body would be visible. Or else, some trace of passage. Grass bent over. Twig snapped. Anything. He looked for the glint of a rifle. The weapon had to be there somewhere. Surely

it wouldn't have been dropped in the water. Even the Babb Brothers would know better than that.

B. J. looked at Joe again, this time grinning. As though to say: "You dumb ox! Can't you see that? Anybody with one bad eye ought to be able—."

Exasperating! B. J. pointed again. Joe stared. He followed the amorphous gray reflections in the pool. The stems of grass at the water's edge. *B. J.,* he thought, *your eyes must have been made a lot sharper in the Louisiana bayous than mine were in the Wyoming mountains. Well, why not? This resembles a bayou more than a mountain...*"

Still, all eyes had to be made of the same stuff that—.

And then, when mind and eye finally coalesced, he saw a small object that had one special, revealing characteristic nothing else had in this environment.

Of course! He should have seen it at once, as B. J. had. He had *trained* himself to pick out the unusual in the commonplace.

A straight line.

He peered again to make sure he had made no mistake. Everything in the shadows seemed to meld, to become a morass of shapes that blurred as he watched. But clearly now he saw a straight line just above the water.

B. J. looked at Joe again, then very carefully took a step forward. At the same time, his eyes did another 360-degree scan of the surroundings. He checked every limb, every tree trunk, every clump of grass. Then he pointed down into the grass just back from the edge of the pool.

That's when Joe saw the rifle butt. B. J. reached down, picked up the rifle, and handed it to Joe. Then, craning his neck, he looked back into the water.

Joe took the weapon, an old battered Winchester, and placed it farther back in the grass. Then, stepping forward, he followed B. J's. fixed gaze once more, and saw a black snorkel tube protruding from the water just under a grassy overhang.

B. J. glanced at Joe with what could only be described as a scheming, diabolical look. He lay down his rifle. Moving slowly, he reached down into the grass beside his feet and retrieved a mixture of loose sand and gravel. Lifting a fistful of it, he knelt and reached out over the edge of the bank.

Joe almost exploded with laughter. And curses. Why hadn't he thought of that? A typical Joe Muck type of trick! He could learn from this ranger. Well, he consoled himself, if he had seen the snorkel first, he'd have beaten B. J. to this trick.

Cupping his hand carefully, in the shape of a funnel, B. J. poured a narrow stream of sand and gravel down the open end of the snorkel.

Joe stood back.

The water erupted explosively as a coughing, choking figure came to the surface, flailing wildly. B. J. pounced directly on him, and the ensuing moments produced a more splashing, banging, lunging, grunting combat between two human beings than Joe had ever seen.

B. J. attempted to seize the figure in an immobilizing grip, but the writhing, the savage elbowing, the twisting and turning, made that impossible. Each landed blows on the other, one offensive, the other defensive, coughing, choking, fighting for life.

Joe looked for a way to interfere, to enter the fray, to seek some advantage and seize the villain. But he knew he would only confuse the matter if he jumped in and tried to take the fight from B. J.

From what he could tell, in the mêlée of flying fists and splashing water, B. J. seemed to be doing all right by himself. The ranger landed telling blows that seemed the more vicious for each accompanying *SLAP!* of water. B. J. managed to push the head beneath water, if only for a moment, to exacerbate the choking from sand and gravel. The man erupted from the pool and sent an elbow viciously under B. J.'s chin. This sent B. J. backward, momentarily off balance. He staggered, recovered, ducked under the water and seized the culprit's

arm in a twisting maneuver, resulting in a sputtering howl of pain. With a massive effort, B.J. shouldered the body and heaved it up toward the bank—like a Cajun, Joe thought, heaving an alligator up on shore.

Joe reached out and clamped the man with a vise-like grip, worked him around and got him to his feet, then twisted the arm behind the back. Another howl of pain, and the adversary subsided.

"Okay," Joe barked at once, looking at the quarry but directing his question at B. J. "Which Babb is this?"

"Duke, I think."

Joe released the pressure on the arm long enough for B. J. to grasp the wrists and tie them behind Duke's back with a reinforced plastic cord. Then they spun him around.

"Where are the others?" Joe snapped.

Duke dropped his head and said nothing.

Joe flipped the chin up. "I'm speaking to you, dumb boy. How many of your brothers came with you?"

Duke spoke, coughing out sand in the process. "I don't know nuthin'. What you talkin' 'bout?"

"I'm talking about Smoke and Winnie. Where are they?"

B. J. inserted: "And Blue. There are four of them all together."

Duke Babb looked at Joe with fierce eyes. "Ah don' know what th' hell you talkin' 'bout. I wuz jus' tryin' to git a peaceful swim..."

Joe: "With your goddamned clothes on? We'd better get this straight right now, you slinking bastard. I got a thing against murder—a real thing. 'Specially when you're trying to kill guests from foreign countries. They come here expecting American hospitality and you sling a bullet at 'em. I ought to take you over there and drown you right now."

As he talked, Joe watched Duke's eyes. For the most part, they remained lowered. Joe towered above the slumped figure, which meant that only with difficulty could he peer into those eyes and find what he sought. Ever so small an indication. A surreptitious glance up the creek.

Perhaps one without Joe's training would have missed it...the unconscious movement of an eyeball in the direction of—what? The other brother? Or brothers?

Joe needed nothing more. He grasped the collar of Duke's soaked shirt and pushed him forward. At the same time, he caught B. J.'s eyes and, by moving his own glance upstream, said, in effect, we're going upstream, please pick up those rifles and cover me.

"Now, Duke," Joe said, pushing him unceremoniously forward. "You're going to go in front of me. The ranger has a gun on you and is ready to shoot anyone we run into. It would just be a helluva lot easier on you if we knew where we were going. You and your brothers are accessories to a very serious crime."

He paused for effect. Then, roving over the inner workings of human nature, he lied. "You killed one of the ranking officers of the UN Environment Programme."

Duke suddenly jumped up and down in glee. "Oh, good! Good! God damn! I got 'im! I *got* the sonbitch! Shit, man, ever' hunter in the whole country will be glad. I'll be a hero. Ain't you a hunter? Ain't you glad? Don't you know what he was after? Huh? He wanted to take our guns away from us!"

"Yes, you'll be a real hero, Duke. Everybody will just be so fuckin' *proud* of you. You won't be able to stand it.

Now, where are the rest of your brothers? We want to thank them, too."

Duke lapsed into silence. Joe pushed him on, through a grassy thicket, under some tall cottonwoods, and around the end of a fallen cottonwood trunk. By that time, they had arrived back at the main pool and terraces below Havasu Falls. This meant they had to raise their voices to be heard above the roar of the falling water.

"You expect to get off easy?" Joe asked Duke, searching again for a signal. "You think public opinion is in your favor?"

Duke said nothing.

"Man, you just killed a foreign dignitary inside an Indian reservation right next to a national Park. That's two or three *Federal* crimes. If that doesn't mean the gallows, I don't know what the hell does."

This statement had a visible effect on Duke. His eyes darted from Joe to B. J., then made another of those surreptitious, almost imperceptible, glances, this time to the east, toward the sandy-floored tributary canyon that joined Havasu Canyon at the falls.

Joe glanced quizzically up the tributary and then toward B. J., who said: "Old mine up there."

To which Joe responded: "Oh, there is, is there? An old mine, you say? Well, what do you know about that?"

Joe turned his head to look across the pool beneath the falls and up at the trail where the rest of the group had been. He saw that Chala and the UN group had gone. The rangers remained—Mozo, Cynthia, Eddie and Dalton, spread out along the trail. They stood looking down on Joe, B. J. and Duke. Joe fathomed that they didn't know yet whether to cheer or come running to help. They apparently hadn't seen anyone else, or they would have indicated that. He hoped that the appearance of Duke as a captive would tell them that he and B. J. had things under control and did not need help.

Then Joe turned and looked up the canyon. There, about two hundred yards away, against the right wall, he saw a mine dump, distinctive for being light-colored in a dark gray canyon. The mine opening appeared to be about ten feet above the stream bed.

"So there's an old mine up there," Joe said again, for Duke's benefit. "You don't really say?"

He gave Duke an abrupt shove in the direction of the mine.

Duke stumbled forward. The pond water on his face and head had now been replaced by perspiration. Though the sun had gone, the deep and narrow canyon held the heat like a furnace. Joe and B. J., of course, also dripped with perspiration.

Joe paced himself and Duke with slow, if uneven and sometimes staggering, steps. B. J. remained behind, Duke's rifle slung over his shoulder, his own rifle held at the ready. His eyes remained fixed on the mine ahead. He could not see into the opening. Joe had directed him not to expose himself in front of the mine entrance

Thus, they walked along the right wall. "We're getting closer, Duke," said Joe.

No response.

"Is there anyone in there, Duke?"

No answer.

"'Cause if there is, he or they are gonna come out any minute now with guns blazin'. And they won't give a goddamn who they hit. You know that, don't you, Duke?"

No reply.

The sound of Havasu Falls had now subsided, diffused by echoes from the walls, muffled by distance and the corner of a high wall. The sound of their footsteps on the sand, though not loud, did get some amplification and reverberation in this natural echo chamber.

"They should be able to hear our footsteps now, Duke", Joe continued. "I'd guess it's only a matter of seconds now. We're within range. I guess you can see that, can't you?"

Duke scowled, lifted his head, looked at the mine, then back at B. J. Sweat stood out in multiple beads on his temples.

Joe went on, half snarling. "What kinds of rifles do they have, Duke? Winchesters? Remingtons? Have you ever seen what one of those slugs does to a man? You've seen what it does to a deer at a hundred yards. What about a man? At twenty yards? You may know in a minute ..."

He watched Duke, as the head sank, then lifted again. "Oh, Jesus *Christ!*" Duke muttered. "Shut the fuck up!"

Directing his voice toward the mine, Duke bellowed as loudly as he could.

"WINNIE! WINNIE! IT'S ME, DUKE. HOLD YOUR FIRE. THEY GOT ME, WINNIE. THEY GOT ME. DON'T TRY NUTHIN'. IT'S THE FEDS!"

Joe stood elated. He now knew how many and who had taken refuge in the cave. Duke had broken. Now for Act II. Duke and Winnie center stage.

"WINNIE! DO YUH HEAR ME? IT'S DUKE. I SAID HOLD YOUR FIRE. THEY GOT ME."

Nothing but silence from the cave.

"I COULDN'T HELP IT, WINNIE. THE WATER THING DIDN'T WORK! I KNEW IT WOULDN'T. I DONE TOL' YUH THAT, FER CHRIST'S SAKE!"

The words echoed eerily between the walls. Then only silence and the vague murmur of the falls behind them.

"WINNIE! GOD DAMN IT! SAY SOMETHIN' ... WELL, I GOT GOOD NEWS. I GOT THE SONBITCH. WHAT D'YUH THINK OF THAT? SMOKE MUSTA MISSED HIM. BUT I GOT 'IM. RIGHT 'TWEEN THE EYES. RIGHT THROUGH THE HAT. WASN'T THAT SOMETHIN'?"

Pause. No response.

"WE'LL BE HEROES, WINNIE. THEY CAIN'T DO NUTHIN' TO US CUZ PUBLIC OPINION'S ON OUR SIDE. YOU KNOW THAT, WINNIE? I SWEAR! NOW

COME ON OUT. AIN'T GOT NUTHIN' TO WORRY ABOUT ... WINNIE?"

After this soliloquy, Joe said quietly to Duke: "He thinks you're lying. He hasn't seen us. Or maybe he saw us coming and left."

"No!" Duke answered. "We had our plan. Only we didn't expect it to turn out this way..."

Joe motioned for B. J. to come forward. When he did, Joe said to Duke: "I'm going to turn you over to the ranger now, Duke. You're not making any headway with Winnie. So I'll get him out of there."

He turned to B. J. "You two stay back here. This won't take long."

With that, Joe took his rifle from his shoulder and got it ready. He stepped forward about ten paces and moved to the left, almost to the center of the canyon.

He aimed at the opening—still clinging to the possibility that Winnie would try to emerge and take a quick pot shot at him. That would force him to shoot off an ear or a finger to stop the man. He would take Winnie alive... He thought of no other alternative.

The moments passed. Still no sound from the cave.

Slowly, Joe aimed at a spot within the chamber, toward the solid limestone wall on the far side. He fired.

The bullet entered the cave and ricocheted with a *ping-nnng! Zing-nnng! Zong-nnng!*

The echoes of the gunshot zigzagged up the canyon, bouncing off the walls, until they faded in the distance.

He waited. Duke watched the mouth of the cave with a mixture of fear and curiosity.

A minute passed. Nothing disturbed the quiet of the canyon ... or the cave.

Joe lifted his rifle again, picked another point on the wall, and fired. *Ping-nnng! Twang-nnng! Zonnk!"*

This time a voice came from the cave. "Ow-www! God damn! You son of a bitch! You filthy son-of-a-*bitch*!"

With that, a rifle came sailing out of the mouth of the cave, hurled with such force that it reached almost to the far wall of the canyon. It clattered into a fallen sandstone boulder and came apart with a loud crash.

Winnie Babb, clad in a pair of coveralls with the sleeves rolled up as high as he could get them, emerged from the cave and slowly walked down the tailings slope and toward the waiting men. B. J. went forward with a reinforced plastic bracelet.

By the time they got back to the main trail, Winnie and Duke had been roped together and walked dejectedly, humiliatingly, in front of B. J. As they started up the trail past Havasu Falls, they encountered Mozo Fernandez and Cynthia Kasbolt. B. J. turned the Babbs over to them. Joe chanced to look up. At the top of the incline, the UN contingent, plus Neff, Angel, Eddie and Dalton, looked down upon them. In front, tall and regal as an emperor, stood Hounto Chala in his sky-blue ceremonial robes and a beaten, battered cowboy hat.

Duke saw it too, and babbled forlornly, half sobbing: "You tol' me I *got* 'im. You said I got that sonbitch. You said so right down there. You did."

Joe said, not taking his eyes off Chala. "I must've lied. But take heart, Duke. You got the hat. Ain't that sumpin'? A little lower and you'da gotten me."

Duke broke down. "Oh, God damn, damn..."

Winnie, though shackled, tried to cuff him with an elbow, muttering in bitter contempt: "You stupid ass!"

Duke shot back: "I hit the hat. I did."

Chala called, motioning them up the trail: "Joseph! Beejay! Venez-ici!"

Joe said to B.J.: "We're being summoned."

The others applauded as Joe and B. J. climbed the trail up to where they stood.

Joe looked at Chala and his robe. "Mon eminence ... Vous voulez faire un entrance royal dans le village, n'est-ce pas?"

Of course, he wants to make a royal entrance, Joe thought. *How else would someone like Hounto Chala enter another village? The village of the Havasupais?*

Joe did not bother to tell him that they still had two miles to go. *If you want to hike in this heat in that robe...*

Chala clutched Joe in one of the most royal of embraces. The group exploded in applause. Chala moved over to B. J. and bestowed upon him an equally royal embrace.

Everyone talked at once. Sam Petrie grabbed Joe's hand, then B. J.'s. "What we owe to you two!"

Dee Dunn bussed Joe on the cheek. "Cheers for the UN!" she said.

Dietrich Deitemeyer came forward, shaking his head in disbelief. "How can we thank you? It has been a fight. A fight! A whamdinger, you say? Can we go in peace, now?"

Joe nodded. "Well, I think so. But stay alert."

Kent Thomas took Joe's and B. J.'s hands. "We saw very little of that. Tonight you two are going to tell all of us what happened down there."

Chala took the head of the procession, placing Joe to his right and B. J. to his left. With that he said, "Allons-y!" The rest shouted; "Allonz-ee!" and up the trail they went, leaving behind the waters of Havasu Creek, falling into one of the most peaceful vales on earth.

Woody Watkins walked up the final switchbacks on the ascent of the Kaibab Trail to the South rim, cooled by soft breezes in the shadows. Perspiration poured down his neck. As he broke out into the sunlight, the piñon and juniper trees filtered the afternoon rays and highlighted the silhouette of Lee Federico, chief ranger, leaning against the front of his patrol car.

Woody stopped to catch his breath. "Whew! Lee, I'm so glad you're here. There's been a terrible accident!"

Federico did not move.

"Julie and I were standing on the outer edge of the trail, down in the Coconino. This pack train comes along and one of the mules got spooked and shifted in the trail." He put his face in his hands. "Oh, it was awful! Before I knew it, she was gone ... Such a wonderful, wonderful girl ... And to think, I hired her."

Lee Federico stood with his arms folded, saying nothing.

"Lee?" Woody said. "Well, you've got to get someone down there to pick up the remains. It was awful."

Only the breezes through the needles of piñons answered.

"Well, you're not blaming *me?* God, I couldn't help it. She was gone practically before I knew what...was...going...on... Lee?"

Their eyes met and fixed for a long moment.

"What's the matter, Lee? Is something wrong?"

Lee's face remained as though fixed in concrete, devoid of emotion, no hint of the thoughts behind his glacial eyes. Finally, he spoke, his voice an ominous bass.

"Yes, Woody. We've seen your bank account."

This statement affected Woody like a thunderbolt. He seemed to freeze. His face went white. His eyes locked onto Lee's. His jaw dropped, as though he had something to say....

No words emerged.

Lee said nothing more, standing as solid and unmoving as a cliff of the Redwall limestone.

Woody focused on the patrol car. Lee would take him away in it. Not back to his office overlooking the piñon-juniper community of trees at headquarters. Not to his home among the ponderosa pines.

To a lonely cell in the local jail.

Woody stepped backward, his eyes still locked on Lee's in an uncomprehending, quizzical stare. Then he broke the gaze and moved his head to the side, shifted his body, and turned his back to Lee.

For a long moment, he stood as though dumfounded, confused, searching for something to say.

He took a step toward the trail head. Then another. In a few moments he found himself walking slowly toward the trail. He did not look back, but he must have guessed that Lee Federico had not moved.

In this taut silence Woody walked away, back in the direction he had come. He stepped onto the trail and began the descent, back down the narrow switchbacks...

Lee watched him drop out of sight down the pathway, watched the head bobbing slowly, and made no move to apprehend him...

Watkins descended slowly, as though unseeing, unsure of his footing. His eyes had glazed, darting from rim to trail to canyon, not seeming to see anything. And not looking back.

He made the descent of the switchbacks through the Kaibab limestone and continued to walk slowly, hesitatingly, where the trail straightened along the base of the cliff. His head dropped. He moved like a robot, placing one foot ahead of the other, now seeming not to see much else than the trail.

After this had gone on for perhaps ten minutes, his pace slowed and stopped. He sensed the presence of some other human beings.

Slowly, he looked up.

A few steps away, Julie Baxter and I faced him in the trail.

Behind sat Rusty Gorman on a ledge, holding the reins of his horse. Behind that stood the other horses and the pack horse with the canvas body bag.

For a moment, no one said anything. Then I spoke.

"We heard her and lowered a rope to her, Woody."

Not a flicker in Woody's eyes. Not a shiver of shoulders or hands.

"This is a very brave woman, Woody. I'm glad you got to know her, however briefly. She's a kind of standard against which other men and women can be measured. She's very brilliant at logic and deductions... don't you think, Woody?"

Silence.

"She came to the same conclusions Buck and I did, Woody. Buck is not far behind us with Smoke and Blue in tow. We hear by radio that Joe Muck and B. J. have Duke

and Winnie in custody in Supai. They'll squeal, of course, and spill all the beans."

I paused and looked out over the canyon vastness. "Your little plan, so carefully put together with the Babb Brothers, has only made a martyr of Chala. Yes, Woody, he's alive and well. You got the little Thai, but you made a hero of him, too. Kathi's doing stories on all these people."

Woody had not moved.

"And now," I went on, "she'll do a final story on you. And it will play around the U.S., Europe, Africa—the world. How the fur trade bought you. How Senator Sweeney tempted you to greater heights. Julie told us about all that. Oh, the Senator will be very proud of you, Woody. He once called you his protégé? What a badge of honor. Bright-eyed, did he say? And brilliant? Going places? Doing things?"

For a moment the scene seemed like a tableau in an *ouvrage de cire,* molded in wax at Madame Tussaud's, with none of the players moving, scarcely even breathing.

"Well, Woody," I went on, "you went places and did things, all right. You've tarnished his name. But he'll say that you were only a minor functionary of some remote government bureau, and he won't quite recall who you were..."

I looked at the ground for a moment, then back at the limp and bedraggled figure in the trail.

"The game is over," I said. "You've lost whatever you sought, Woody. That promising career has come to an end. You didn't want the money, did you? Just fame... And power... Oh yes, indeed. Power. No matter what."

Woody moved. They couldn't have stopped him, not even with a fast lunge. He turned outward and leaped up on the wall at the edge of the trail, at the edge of the abyss. He stopped, wavering, ready to leap—.

"Go on!" I shouted. "*Jump!*"

Woody stood poised, bent, ready but shocked by the word.

"Jump! *That* will admit your guilt to Senator Sweeney. He'll be proud of you...taking the coward's way out. Don't you think? Any other man would have *stayed,* fought these ridiculous charges, shifted the blame to someone else. You could say you were set up, of course. A sting operation. There are lots of possibilities. Aren't there, Woody?"

The bedraggled figure teetered at the edge. He leaned forward and almost fell, then reeled backward. His hand went to his head. His eyes, blurring his vision, tried to focus.

"If you lose, you'll get off in ten years for good behavior. You know that. And if you win? Think of that! The Senator will be more proud of you than ever. You fought the stupid bureaucracy and won. You made every hunter stand up proudly and take notice to the danger of people like Chala. See what you accomplished? See what more you could accomplish?... If you weren't a coward... Go on. Jump!"

Woody stepped back in the trail, turned, and started walking uphill.

They held back...letting him go.

A white-throated swift, with powerful tapered wings, soared by in a dive through the air, and disappeared hundreds of feet below.

I said: "Lee will be waiting."

We walked forward. Behind us, Rusty rose and led the horses up the trail.

The rays of the rising sun tinted the tops of the inner canyon buttes and mesas with a rich and gentle gold.

A white-breasted nuthatch worked its way up and down the twisted trunk of a juniper tree at the rim, searching the bark for insects. An Abert squirrel, its bushy gray tail touched with white, bounded across a limestone glade and leaped up into a piñon tree in search of seeds.

Joe and Julie paused at the head of the Kaibab Trail, backpacks and sleeping bags strapped to their shoulders, looking out over the shadowy vastness of the canyon.

Joe said: "I can't understand how Lee Federico could give you the time off to take me to the North Rim..."

"Time off?" she countered. "I'm the inner canyon ranger! A few cuts, scratches and bruises, but I'm still in one piece."

"Then this is official duty?"

"It certainly is. Lee said that any VIP who helps take criminals the way you did in Supai deserves a little special attention. Like going on patrol with the ranger."

"Well, I've got to tell Lee I appreciate that."

"And besides," she said, "it was nice of Barry to give you time off."

"Oh, he was happy to," Joe responded. "Sam Petrie insisted on taking him to Supai. So that's where they've gone. Accompanied by Buck, of course."

"What a trio *that* will be!"

"You said it." Joe reflected for a moment. "You know, that's kinda what Barry said about us. About you and me."

"What?"

"What a pair you two will make."

She said: "I must tell Barry I appreciate that. Besides, this trip will give you time to tell me all about what happened in Supai. You've got to tell the whole story from the beginning."

"That's funny," he said.

"What's funny?"

"Well, I used to bug Barry to tell me all about *his* adventures."

"You're a lot like Barry."

"What are you saying? That's the biggest compliment anyone could pay me. You can't mean it."

"I do mean it."

Joe checked the straps on his pack. "He said we'd make a good pair, huh?"

Julie looked at him and grinned. "Well, that depends."

"Depends? On what?"

"Your friend in Laramie."

"Her?" he answered. "She's still in the mall."

Julie laughed. "Do you know what you look like in that hat?"

Two bullet holes had been shot through it. The fabric had been crushed. In all, it looked like the most battered and tattered cowboy hat ever worn into the Grand Canyon.

He grinned back at her. "A gift," he said. "From an old African friend of mine!"

"He's going to miss it."

"No he's not. I bought another one and gave it to him."

She held up her palm. "Allons-y?"

He slapped her palm, saying: "Allons-y!"

They set off down the trail. The switchbacks zigged and zagged in morning shadows. Beyond, the sun had begun to brighten the yellow cliffs and promontories of the Coconino sandstone. As they descended, the breezes along the rim sang a gentle song through the needles of the piñon pines.

Shortly afterward, a mule deer and her month-old fawn emerged from the forest. She looked around, wiggling her ears and twitching her tail. Then they, too, started slowly down the trail.

✦ ✦

About the Author

Ann Livesay is that rare combination of geologist, author, and scientific researcher who takes readers where few other writers have gone—deep into dangerous places worldwide. She has worked in these places, photographed them, and written about them in 22 nonfiction books coauthored with her husband, Myron Sutton. In the Barry Ross International Mysteries, as one reader said, you get the trip without the hassle of airports, taxis and baggage. Ann Livesay brings her skills directly to readers, with authenticity of locale guaranteed. She takes you in, with bold and daring suspense, and knows how to get you back out...maybe.

To purchase **The Chala Project** *or other exciting Barry Ross mysteries, visit your local bookstore.*

Additional information about the author is on our Web site at http://www.silverriver.com. If you would like to be notified when new volumes in the Barry Ross International Mystery Series are available, please write to Silver River and you will be put on our mailing list.

Also in this Series

The Isis Command
Death In the Amazon
The Madman of Mount Everest

(in preparation):

The Dinkum Deaths: Murder on the Great Barrier Reef

✦ ✦

Coming soon to your local bookstore...

THE DINKUM DEATHS:
Murder on the Great Barrier Reef

(Barry Ross has come to Cairns, Australia, to solve two murders on Dinkum Island, part of the Great Barrier Reef. One of the scientists who worked with the dead men has disappeared, and when Joe and Julie Muck arrive, they are dispatched to find him. The trail leads into the Strzelecki Desert in Sturt National Park, in central Australia. They must find a shabby character named Geoff Billabong (obviously a fake name) working on the dingo fence, part of a system to confine the movements of wild dogs called dingos. Joe and Julie stop at Cameron Corners, where Joe stands in South Australia and drives a golf ball across New South Wales into Queensland. From there Joe and Julie head east.)

Chapter Eighteen

Joe drove their pickup along the dirt road that parallels the dingo fence. Sturt National Park stretched in all directions, its red sand dunes and mulga forests shimmered as though being steeped in boiling water.

"Must be 48 today," Julie commented, wiping her brow.

"That's 110 degrees," Joe said. "Put another ice cube down my back. I don't see how those dragon lizards take it."

"They perch in trees," Julie responded.

"That wouldn't help me," he said.

"You're not a reptile," she replied.

The dust didn't help. Their perspiration turned brown. Lines formed on their faces and down their necks.

Ten minutes later, their search for Geoff Billabong ended. He stood beside a post, pliers gripping two strands of wire, pulling and tightening. As they drove up and stopped, he turned and mopped his brow.

They got out, expecting a friendly "Hoi myte," but got nothing more than an indifferent scowl. The worker fit the description all right. Sandy curled hair, always dirty, blue shorts turning mud color, old sandals chipped and scuffed, and a ripped tee shirt showing 4XXXX Beer. To block out the scorching sun, he wore a ragged fiber hat.

As they approached, he turned back to his work.

"Geoff?" Joe asked.

The man said nothing.

"We're from Amurrika," Joe offered, giving it an Australian pronunciation. "G-day, myte."

No response.

Julie asked: "Is this the dingo fence everybody's been telling us about?"

No response.

With this, Joe pulled out his chief weapon. "We got a couple ice cold Four Xes in the truck."

The man's hands stopped moving. His head slowly turned around as he laid eyes on them for the first time.

"Thet so?" he asked.

"Yeh," said Joe, lapsing into the lingo, "Motty keld 'n tysty nthis yer desert 'eat. We got some questions we'd loik t'esk ye."

Billabong pulled a foul blue rag out of his pocket and wiped his brow, saying: "Ye godda deal."

Grabbing the cooler they repaired to the shade of a sand hill spider flower tree. Passing around the beers, Joe started out: "We's workin' on the reef off Cairns and lookin' fer a myte."

Billabong took a big slug of beer, part of which streamed down his chin. "Yeh?"

"You used to work fer 'im. A biologist. Did some ree-search on the corals of Dinkum Island. Ring a bell?"

Geoff said nothing, but the drop of his head answered "Yes."

"'Bout two, three years ago?"

Nodding of the head.

Julie asked very simply: "What was his name?"

Billabong took another slug and asked: "He in trouble?"

Joe answered. "Nope. We just want t'esk him some things 'bout his work."

"You cops?"

"Naw. Just here on holidye. 'Specting to go to the beaches at Sydney when we get throo hyer."

"You ain't cops?"

Julie answered, lying. "We take pictures, sell 'em in magazines."

Geoff scowled again. "You ain't publishin' nuttin' on me?"

Joe shook his head vigorously. "Naw, mon. We looking fer this other chap to find out 'bout the Great Barrier Reef. That's all. No big deal."

Geoff: "He ain't hyer no more."

"We'd like to go talk with 'im 'bout the fishes and such. Know where he is?"

"Cottlesloe."

"Where's that?"

"On the beach."

"Where?"

"Perth."

Joe snorted. "Aw, shit, mon. We got t'keep on goin' t'other side o' this hyer continent?"

Julie persisted. "What's his name?"

Geoff looked at the cooler. She brought out another beer and opened it. He took a long swig, then looked at the cooler again.

She brought out a sandwich. He took it.

Then he spoke in a low tone. "Peter Murray."

With that, he took his beer and sandwich, went back to the dingo fence, set them down, and picked up his pliers again.

Joe looked at Julie. They got in the truck and drove away.

A flight of corellas shrieked as the birds flapped overhead, their white wings glistening in the desert sun. Beneath a Grevillea tree a low-slung shingle-back lizard wiggled slowly away in the shadows.

(In preparation)
© *Ann Livesay*

Colophon

The text of *The Chala Project* is set in 11.5 point Garamond3 on 12.5 point leading. Chapter titles are Post Antigua,with special pages set in the RotisSemiSerif and Post Antigua families.

The text stock is 60 lb recycled paper. It is acid-free for archival durability, and it meets or exceeds all guidelines set forth by the U. S. Environmental Protection Agency for recycled content and use for post-consumer waste. The binding is Perfect Bind.

The cover, text and special character design and production are by Dan Schiffer, Digimedia, 14004 SE 23rd Circle, Vancouver, WA 98683, 360-885-3701. All cover images are derived from copyrighted photographs of the author.

The book was produced on an Apple Macintosh G3 using Adobe InDesign.

Trademarks: Apple and Macintosh are registered trademarks of Apple Computer, Inc. InDesign is a registered trademark of Adobe Systems, Inc.